René Chang

Read other books by René Chang

Scalpel in the Sand -
Memoirs of a Surgeon in Saudi Arabia

Watergate - The Political Asassination

René Chang

René Chang

UFT Press Ltd
First published in Great Britain by UFT Press 2012

http://uftpress.com

Copyright © René Chang, 2012

The rights of René Chang to be identified as the Author of the Work has been asserted by him in accordance with the Copyright, Design and Patents Act 1988

All rights reserved. Apart from any use permitted under UK copyright law, no part of this publication may be reproduced, stored in a retrieval system, or transmitted, in any form or by any means, without the prior written permission of UFT Press.

A CIP catalogue record for this title is available from the British Library

Copyright © 2010 Rene Chang

All rights reserved.

ISBN - 13:987-0-9569119-3-3

Know your enemy and know yourself,

you will win every battle.

Sunzi, *Art of War* (BC 600).

'Selflessness' is the greatest asset a person

can have during a time of crisis.

Richard M Nixon, *Six Crises* (1962).

I disapprove of what you say, but I will defend

to the death your right to say it.

Evelyn Beatrice Hall, *Friends of Voltaire* (1906).

AUTHOR'S NOTE

This is a political novel about the Watergate scandal. While it is based on the incidents arising from the scandal, the storyline here is a figment of my imagination. Some historical persons feature in my story but their parts in it are not attributable to any historical fact and do not have any historical validity.

Pinyin is used for the romanization of Chinese names. The two exceptions are Chiang Kai-shek and Sun Yat-sen as these names in pinyin (Jiang Jieshi and Sun Yixian) are not easily recognized by many.

Notes provides the reader with more background information as the historical events in the story happened some forty years ago. They are separated from the text in order not to slow down the plot. In the print version, they are denoted by superscripted numerals in the text. In the eBook version, there are hyperlinks to the relevant note. Hyperlinks can be identified as they are underlined in blue. At the end of each note, clicking on <Return to Start Point> will bring the reader back to his/her starting point before jumping to the notes. This is a technological innovation not possible with the print version. If you would like to read footnotes on a topic that had not been included please write to me at renechang@btinternet.com. New notes will be added to the next editi

CAST OF MAIN CHARACTERS

Historical

Bernstein, Carl. - *The Washington Post* reporter

Bradshaw (Bradlee), Ben - Executive Editor *The Washington Post*

Dean, John - White House Special Counsel

Ehrlichman, John - White House Assistant

Haldeman, Bob - White House Chief of Staff

Hunt, Howard - White House 'plumber'

Kissinger, Henry - National Security Advisor

Liddy, Gordon - White House 'plumber'

Mao Zedong - Chairman Communist Party of China

Nixon, Richard Milhous - 37th President of USA

Woodward, Bob - *The Washington Post* reporter

Zhou Enlai - Premier of China

Fictitious

Cato, Nick - Chair-elect of China Lobby

Cornfield, Sarah - *LA Times* reporter

Cornfield Jack, - Sarah's father, ex-Marine Intelligence

Cunningham, Sarah - pseudonym of Sarah Cornfield

Defoe, Big Bill - Chair of China Lobby

Holmberg, Jacob - Senior FBI officer

Lieberman, Jerome 'Nuts' - White House 'plumber'

Mitford Robert - Supreme Commander, Templar Knights

CONTENTS

AUTHOR'S NOTE vi

CAST OF MAIN CHARACTERS vii

CONTENTS ix

ACKNOWLEDGEMENTS xi

PROLOGUE 1

CHAPTER 1 - PING PONG DIPL0MACY 3

CHAPTER 2 - CHINA LOBBY 9

CHAPTER 3 - THE PLOT 19

CHAPTER 4 - THE NIXON PLAN 28

CHAPTER 5 - NIXON VISITS CHINA 40

CHAPTER 6 - PREPARING THE TRAP 45

CHAPTER 7 - SALT SUMMIT 53

CHAPTER 8 - SPRINGING THE TRAP 55

CHAPTER 9 - SARAH CORNFIELD 64

CHAPTER 10 - THE ASSIGNMENT 70

CHAPTER 11 - SARAH IN WASHINGTON 75

CHAPTER 12 - LUCKY BREAK 80

CHAPTER 13 - SARAH MEETS NIXON 90

CHAPTER 14 - HOTTING UP	90
CHAPTER 15 - DEEP THROAT	109
CHAPTER 16 - MUSINGS ON THE FOURTH ESTATES	113
CHAPTER 17 - THE COUP DE *GRÂCE*	117
EPILOGUE	131
NIXON - A BRIEF BIOGRAPHY	133
NOTES	142
BIBLIOGRAPHY	175
ABOUT THE AUTHOR	177

ACKNOWLEDGEMENTS

Grateful thanks are due to Rosa Goldthorpe and Annette Fitch for checking the manuscript. Of course any remaining errors, factual or typographic are my responsibility

René Chang

PROLOGUE

President Nixon had the dubious distinction to be the first US President to resign from office. He had won two Vice-Presidential elections with President Eisenhower and two Presidential elections. In 1972 when he was re-elected for a second term he won by a landslide of 60.7 per cent of the popular vote, beating the democratic candidate Senator George McGovern by 18 million votes and winning in 49 of 51 states, a historical first. He was also the first US President to have a clean sweep of all of the Southern States at a single election.

Yet Nixon had to resign in 1974 following the Watergate charges.

Was the US electorate that fickle? Or were the voters manipulated? Was it a power play enacted in Washington DC?

What were the charges arising from Watergate? Abuse of presidential power featured universally on the charge sheets of the press, media and courts.

Did Nixon do anything that was spectacularly out of character with those by other US Presidents?

President Johnson 'manufactured' the Gulf of Tonkin Incident[1] to escalate the Vietnam War. President Kennedy was complicit in the assassination of the Catholic President Ngo Dinh Diem[2] of South Vietnam. Then there were the Iran-

Contra[3] scandal of President Reagan, and in more recent years, the infamous 'yellowcake'[4] and the weapons of mass destruction (WMD)[5] of President GW Bush.

I would venture that the above are worse examples of abuse of presidential power and of lying to the electorate and the world than anything related to Watergate. Yet none of those US Presidents had to resign.

Through the work of Richard Dawkins, we now know of the power of memes[6]. Once a particular line of thinking goes viral, there is no stopping the clamour for investigations, or the volume of writings along the lines of the meme. The whole idea takes on a momentum of its own. In this the fourth estate bears great responsibilities.

I am not a particular fan of Nixon, and I do not deny that Watergate happened. However, in researching for this political thriller, I found many inconsistencies and I became more and more convinced that there is at least one other possibility that was never investigated or suspected.

Examples of glossed-over important details are that the Watergate conspirators were arrested on their THIRD[7] attempt at breaking into the Watergate complex. The dollar notes with consecutive serial numbers and the information about Howard Hunt in the address books of TWO of the Cuban conspirators that led investigations into the White House seem contrived. It looks as if the conspirators were seeking to be arrested with incriminating evidence pointing in a certain direction. Why were the ex-CIA 'professionals' so incompetent?

CHAPTER 1 - PING PONG DIPLOMACY

It was early April 1971. The cherry blossoms of the sakura-lined avenues were in full bloom. Petals from dead blossoms carpeted the pavements and the air was filled with the scent of the cherry blossoms. The Thirty-first World Table Tennis Championship[1] in Nagoya, Japan was winding down. It was the penultimate day of the tournament. For the first time in years, a team from the People's Republic of China was participating in the contest which was being closely fought.

Glenn Cowan[2] of the American team emerged from the stadium, bleary eyed, nursing a sore head from a drinking bout the previous evening. He had no match to play until the next day. He yawned and stretched and then swore under his breath, 'Shit, I must have missed the team bus. I'll have to wait another half an hour before the next bus arrives and I am already shattered.'

Just then a member of the Chinese team turned up. He was well turned out in a smart scarlet track suit with the gold five-star emblem across his chest. 'Hi', he said to Cowan, 'would you like a lift back to the village? Our team bus will be here in minutes.'

Glenn was taken by surprise at the offer from the Chinese team player. He had understood from the Department of State's briefing that it was highly unlikely that the Chinese team would be friendly, much less to offer a bus ride back to the competitors' village. Cowan thought, 'I am knackered and could kill for a bed. I can't see any harm in taking up this offer.'

He was quite unaware of the implication of the gesture and his acceptance of the invitation. He looked up and uttered a gasp as he recognized that it was Zhuang Zedong[3], a Chinese contender for the world championship, who had approached him. Cowan had read about him and seen him play in one of the previous rounds a couple of days ago. He had a most beguiling serve.

Zhuang Zedong did not have a service like that of his compatriots[4]. He held the ping pong bat in the pen-holder position and was able to serve in a most beguiling way with a flick of his hand, in a variation of the dual-sided offence. It had always been assumed that he had learnt his serve from his mentor, the great Wang Chuanyao with the active encouragement of his coach Fu Qifang. Zhuang Zedong had been a world champion several times, in 1961, 1963 and 1965 and most players held him in awe. It was therefore a great surprise that Cowan was able to meet face to face with this great player.

The bus for the Chinese team pulled up and Cowan hopped onto the bus which was full of Chinese players chatting noisily. The chatter stopped when they saw him. There was a mix of men and women. He thought the Chinese women players seemed very young for their age. They looked youthful, with their bobbed hair and pony tails. None of them seemed to be wearing any make-up. It was all rather strange for Cowan who was used to American women who vied to look mature and sexy with their elaborate hair-dos and make-up. The women also looked like young boys. This, he soon gathered, was due to the fact that they all had small breasts, another difference from the buxom American female.

All the Chinese players smiled at him. Glenn Cowan felt distinctly disorientated. The friendliness of the Chinese was not something he had been briefed about. He had expected them to at most tolerate him as a passenger on their bus. Several of them came up close to admire his long curly locks. Cowan dressed very unconventionally. In fact, he would have passed as a 1960s hippy if he was not with the US table tennis team. He had on a pair of loose fitting bell-bottomed Levis and sneakers. His table tennis shoes would normally be in his shoe bag, but they were in his room in the players' village as he was not playing that day.

The bus pulled off and they were on their way to the players' village. The next thing that happened put Cowan in a most embarrassing position. Zhuang Zedong, approached him and presented him with a most exquisitely embroidered silk brocade of the Huangshan[5] Mountains. Cowan murmured, 'Xie xie' (thank you), one of the few Mandarin phrases that he had picked up from his mates in Los Angeles Chinatown, where he habitually went to have a quick helping of his favourite duck noodles. Cowan realized that he had nothing of value on him that could pass as a present.

He then remembered the red, white and blue T-shirt in his shoulder bag. It was one of his favourite from years ago. It had the lyrics of the Beatles song, 'Let it be' printed on its back. He loved the T-shirt as he thought it was really cool to have the words of his favourite song on his back. As he did not have anything else on him, he took it out gingerly. To his relief, it was still fresh from its last wash a day ago as he had not worn it since. He folded it carefully and gave the T-shirt to his Chinese counterpart. He could not help murmuring, 'This is my present to you. It is very precious as it is my favourite T-shirt.' The cost value of his T-shirt was very little compared to the embroidered silk brocade, but emotionally it was priceless to Cowan. Thankfully, the Chinese player displayed the appropriate appreciation of the priceless gift from Cowan. He initially refused the T-shirt as it was a personal item, but then said, 'The very personal gift represents the bonds of deep friendship between the Chinese and American peoples.' Everyone on the bus applauded at that moment and Cowan felt consoled, having made a huge personal sacrifice.

That evening, Chairman Mao[6] heard of the incident and was very pleased at the development. He summoned Zhou Enlai and other leading comrades from the Foreign Ministry and gave instructions to extend an invitation to the American table tennis team to visit China.

The American team, much surprised and taken aback by the turn of events, were thrilled by the opportunity to be the first Americans to set foot officially on Chinese soil. President Nixon, who was following developments closely, was just as surprised but readily gave his approval as he saw it as the possible opening between the two countries – a major foreign policy initiative that he had been working towards for some years. That night President Nixon and his National Security Advisor, Professor Henry Kissinger drank a toast to the ultimate success of this very dangerous change in American foreign policy.

The American team arrived at Guangzhou (Canton) by train from Hong Kong a few days after the tournament. They were stared at by the Chinese and they stared back. The Chinese were much taken by Glenn Cowan's hippy outfits and also by a woman team member who was wearing a miniskirt. There they boarded the Chinese airliner that took them to Shanghai and then Beijing. The airliner provided excellent service which was at the same time primitive. The Americans were rather amused that tea was served from massive cast iron kettles. It was functional, but not at all elegant.

On the evening of April 15, 1971 there was the customary banquet in the Great Hall of the People. Glenn Cowan and his team members climbed up the wide marble stairs to the banqueting hall. The US team were accompanied by the teams from Canada, Colombia, Britain, and Nigeria. Premier Zhou Enlai was at the top of the stairs to greet his guests.

Zhou was a most charming host. He spoke about the weather with the British team members and to the Canadians he mentioned the contributions of Dr Norman Bethune[7], the Canadian surgeon who assisted and died among the Chinese during the anti-Japanese War. He toasted the president of the US team, saying, 'Your visit has opened a new chapter in the history of the relations between the Chinese and American peoples.' He went on, 'With you having made the start, the peoples of the United States and China in the future will be able to have constant contact.'

At the end of the banquet, Cowan popped up and asked Premier Zhou what he thought of the hippy movement. Zhou said that he did not know much about it. Perhaps the young wanted change, but had not yet found the ways to bring it about. Cowan explained that the hippy movement was very deep and that it represented a whole new way of thinking. Zhou Enlai suggested that more was needed to transform the spirit to a material force to move the world forward. Cowan's mother later sent flowers to Zhou for talking to and educating her son.

The day before the banquet, on April 14, 1971, Nixon had ended most of the trade restrictions between the United States and China.

A couple of days later, during a speech Nixon wished his daughter would be able to visit China. At the end of April, 1971, Nixon at a press conference maintained that one day he would visit China in some capacity. He was slowly introducing the world to his new foreign policy. He was so excited that he was having difficulty in keeping his new policy under wraps, despite the obvious dangers to his political career of a premature leak.

CHAPTER 2 - CHINA LOBBY

'The bastard Nixon, for some time I have felt that he cannot be trusted!' exclaimed Senator William (Big Bill) Defoe, the octogenarian leader of the powerful China Lobby. Big Bill was a big man over seven foot in height and weighed nearly two hundred kilograms. He had a ruddy complexion and steely blue eyes.

He was a colonel with the Flying Tigers[1] in Burma. They flew supplies from Burma to Chongqing, China during the Second World War to break the Japanese blockade. He did no actual flying as the cockpits of the DC3s were too small for his stature. More often than not, he was a passenger in one of these slow but very reliable airplanes. Chongqing was where he had met and developed a long-standing relationship with Chiang Kai-shek and his lovely wife Song Meiling[2]. Being an anti-communist it was natural that he became a firm ally of Generalissimo Chiang. After V-J Day, Big Bill was on the staff of the China Liaison Committee at the same time as General Joseph Stilwell[3]. However, Big Bill opposed the policy of General Stilwell as he was on the side of Generalissimo Chiang.

Big Bill was assigned to the China Liaison Committee for precisely the reason that Chiang had to have his supporters there. Big Bill had known Nixon since 1948, when he had proposed that Nixon be a member of the Committee of Un-American Activities. He had considered Nixon to be his protégé. This would account for his anger and sense of betrayal and hurt.

'That son of a bitch has betrayed me. Recommending and backing him were the biggest errors in my entire political career. All that anti-Commie talk during the 1950s was just a cover for his dastardly plans. I smell a rat. There is definitely something going on between the President and Red China.'

Big Bill had hurriedly called an emergency meeting of the Central Council of the China Lobby. For obvious reason it had another more respectable name – the Council for Human Rights and Democracy (CHRD)[4].

The Council for Human Rights and Democracy was formed during the Second World War by supporters of Generalissimo Chiang Kai-shek, then the President of Nationalist China. It is said to be the brainchild of Song Meiling, wife of the Generalissimo. Educated at Wellesley College, Harvard, before the Pacific War she was conversant with the workings of the US government. The China Lobby was formed to garner support for the Guomindang[5] and to lobby for the encirclement of the communist bloc made up of China and the USSR. Its members were anti-communists who had their heyday in the McCarthy era, weeding out communist agents.

Over the years, as it became less and less likely that the Red China regime of Mao Zedong would be overthrown, the China Lobby lost its high public profile. However, the Lobby had maintained its powerful anti-communist stance by forming clever alliances and coalitions with other right wing power blocs of the United States of America. Its officers were chairmen or members of powerful Congressional or Senatorial committees. It had close links with and had the financial support of all the major defence corporations. It is said that it had links even with the notorious Ku Klux Klan. It was thus a very powerful lobby to promote right wing anti-communist agenda in the United States legislature. Although anti-Semitic in its outlook, it had taken the strategic decision to support Zionist Israel[6] in order that the United States of America could keep a tight hold of the oil resources in the Middle East. Its members had infiltrated the Federal Bureau of Investigations, and the Central Intelligence Agency. It even had spies within the offices of the Chief of General Staff, the highest military authority of the land. Its justification was that it sees itself as the defender of freedom and ultimately of the country. It also had strong links with the Templar Knights[7], another anti-communist secret organization.

'We need to come up with a response, a solution, as Nixon, the motherfucker is about to change the direction of US foreign policy. I present to you the pointers that we have accumulated that indicate that the cunt is up to no good. While there is nothing concrete or definite yet, we cannot afford to be found wanting. Each example on its own seems innocent enough, but taken together, the message is loud and clear. My friends, our country is in grave danger.

'An alarm bell rang in my head when I heard Nixon give his speech in 1967 at the Bohemian Grove before his presidential campaign. He hinted at the need to review

American foreign policy in light of the changes in geopolitics and the rupture between the USSR and Red China. I have also read his article in the journal Foreign Affairs, making similar points.

'Have any of you seen the significance of the mother-selling-whore, Edgar Snow[8], being invited to participate in the October National Day celebrations last year? He was on the podium with Mao. The Chinese do not do things without a purpose. That, my friends, was an important signal.

'The bilateral talks in Warsaw have been reactivated. Walter Stoessel, our ambassador has been seen and photographed with the Chinese ambassador. We thus have the bloody necessary proof. The US and Chinese embassy cars have been reported to be going back and forth. We have to increase and improve our vigilance. We need to activate all our assets; the FBI, the CIA and even the Joint Chiefs and put them on a high state of alert. We cannot afford to be caught on the hop on this occasion', warned Big Bill as he projected several photographs of the US ambassador to Poland hobnobbing with his Chinese counterpart onto the screen affixed to the wall.

'We were caught by surprise by Hungary in 1956 and the Czech Republic in 1968. Those were very bad and dangerous intelligence lapses. We must have our fingers on the pulse and we must learn from our past mistakes.'

'The Chinese have recently invited the US table tennis team to visit China. I think this is a very significant development,' interrupted Nick Cato, Chair of the powerful Congressional

Ways and Means Committee, and next in line to be the Chairman of the Central Council of the China Lobby. Nick was a big Texan, though not as big as Big Bill. He had piercing blue eyes and a crown of brown hair surrounding a bald pate. His high forehead indicated high intelligence. Nick had sided with General Claire Chennault in the dispute between Chiang and General Stilwell on what to do to resist Japan. It had led to the dismissal of General Stilwell from the China theatre.

'But Nixon had bombed Hanoi[9],' piped Henry Prendergast, who was thought to be a bit of a dove and therefore not completely reliable. Henry was a small man and had survived some twenty years of cut-throat Washington politics by a strongly developed propensity for deviousness. His deviousness was the direct result of his intelligence and a strong sense for survival. He could always work out who were the main movers and shakers in any organization. He used his wiles to develop relations with these people so that his own position was protected. His use had been to raise potential problems or objections to ideas generated by the CHRD and provide clever alternatives and 'solutions'. He was also known to be an anti-communist, although a thoughtful one, often playing the role of the devil's advocate. The China Lobby members did not trust him, but he had the protection of Big Bill. Henry's position was secure as long as Big Bill was around.

'Nixon appointed Henry Kissinger the Harvard Jew-boy to be the National Security Council Advisor the day after his inauguration. Kissinger is known to be a Chinese sympathizer and a so-called expert in this new fandangled thing he calls geopolitics. This is high treason. The Jew-boy has pro-Red views. He has his eyes on the long term. If he and Nixon were to pull off the China initiative, I predict that he will have a consultancy to advise on matters Chinese for the big businesses. That motherfucker is in it for the money,' continued Senator (Big Bill) Defoe.

'Between Nixon and Kissinger, the State Department has effectively been cut off from the loop. We are no longer receiving any intelligence from the State Department. In a word, it has dried up. This is a very dangerous situation if we cannot keep our fingers on the national pulse. They are running the goddam show as if the Presidency is a dictatorship. Poor William Rogers, he does not have a clue of what is going on,' continued Bill.

'But the Presidency is a dictatorship. It is just that at present our interests are not being served,' ventured Henry.

'It is not surprising as William Rogers, the prick, is such a nancy. We will change the situation. A mole will be placed in the inner sanctum with Kissinger,' nodded Nick in agreement with Big Bill, but ignoring Henry Prendergast's unworthy contribution, and making his own suggestion.

'What about the shooting of students at Kent State University[10] when they protested against the invasion of Cambodia?' interjected Henry, seemingly oblivious to the rejection of his earlier comments.

'The invasion of Cambodia and the bombing of Hanoi may just be a feint. I don't see any gain from the latter. Except for the military industrial boys who are minting it as each bomb costs $1,200 and we are dropping over a thousand a day. The bombing of Hanoi would cost some $60 million. The Cambodian invasion has failed and the South Vietnam army (ARVN) is not reliable,' observed Nick.

'I am surprised that the Vietcong have not been bombed to the Stone Age,' again quipped Henry.

'Let us get back to the urgent matters at hand. We have to have a response if we fear that Tricky Dickie is about to bring about a major change in US foreign policy. We need to have a set of well-developed plans for the eventuality that he brings about a drastic change in foreign policy,' said Senator (Big Bill) Defoe as he summoned the meeting to order. 'Let me say this. The country is dangerously divided and the reputation of the United States of America will take a severe beating internationally if Nixon's initiatives were to succeed – something we cannot afford.'

'Why don't we take him out politically? Killing him off politically I say will teach him and others a more severe lesson than taking him out physically,' suggested Henry Prendergast.

'That is a brilliant idea, Henry. Depending on how we do it, we may well be uniting the country on an anti-Nixon ticket for the next election, thus killing two birds with a single stone,' said Big Bill approvingly. Although Henry Prendergast could be irritating, he usually saved the day with an excellent suggestion that more often than not would have the approval of the members of the China Lobby.

'Political assassination is a jolly good idea. Let us vote on it. If there is no disagreement, I nominate Nick to be in charge of drawing up the plans to finish off the son of a bitch politically,' repeated Bill approvingly. Henry's suggestion was carried unanimously.

'There must be the utmost secrecy, with multiple cut-outs. No conspiracy theorist must be allowed to find any evidence of our plans.' It was Nick's turn to flesh out the plans.

'I suggest that we focus on the fondness of Nixon and Kissinger for secrecy and his re-election in 1972. From all accounts, Nixon has the habit of going through all options, even the most ridiculous, just to make sure that he has exhausted all possibilities before making a decision. We can make use of this habit to plant incriminating evidence against him. He is also very loyal to his team members; that is why they are so loyal to him in return. Well, at least the leading cabal of aides. He loves to delegate and I hear that there is extremely lax security in recruiting to his team. It seems that a friend of a friend is good enough. There are no thorough security checks. This is surprising for a man with Nixon's perceived reputation. These are weaknesses that we can exploit. Finally, I also have this very little known piece of information – since 1971, Nixon has installed an automatic taping device that automatically records all conversations in the White House, presumably for historical reasons and posterity. I am sure we can make use of this facility at some stage to incriminate Nixon. Nick, don't forget this little gem in your plans,' concluded Big Bill, pleased with his contribution.

'I would suggest leaking some important documents as a trial run to gauge the response of the Nixon team. It is quite easy to prod persons disillusioned with the Vietnam War to leak some important Vietnam War material from say the Brooking Institute or some other think-tank like the Rand Corporation[11]. The trap cannot and must NOT be linked to Nixon's new China policy, otherwise it would be very easy to blame the right wing opposition. We have to run this mission as one from the liberal left, in order to deal Nixon a severe lesson, with little risk of exposure. I have been told on good authority that Nixon, for all his ruthless reputation, has a very lax way of recruiting into the team. Nixon is also fond of delegating. I am sure we can find a way to insinuate a person into the re-election team that will do our bidding and spring the final trap,' continued Big Bill. He had a tendency to repeat what he considered to be important points. It was not a sign of age as he had been doing that ever since he took high public office decades ago.

The dozen or so old men filed out of the Council room.

Nick drew himself up. He was very pleased to be given the task. He liked to work behind the scenes pulling the strings of his vast array of puppets. Nick was a seasoned operator of Washington DC. He had his hands on many of the levers of power. He was known to be extremely devious and ruthless.

It was not without reason that he was also known as the 'Puppet Master'.

The project had to be run by another outfit. This would be the first cut-off. He would use his contacts with the Templar Knights, the red dragon slayers. He liked the symbolism of using the dragon-killing knights to cut off the Red dragon's head.

CHAPTER 3 - THE PLOT

Two days later, at the East Potomac Park Golf Course along the South West Freeway, Nick could be seen playing with one of his cronies. The East Potomac Golf Course was conveniently situated midway between the Capitol building and Foggy Bottom. Its open spaces with cherry blossoms in spring were ideal for frank conversations away from any spook. Another advantage was its lack of popularity among the elite of Washington DC. Unbeknown to any bystander, Nick's companion was not any old crony. With Nick was Robert Mitford, Grand Master and Supreme Commander of the Templar Knights. Robert Mitford was another old China hand. A direct ancestor of his was reputed to have participated in one of the Christian crusades against Saladin in the Middle East. This was how Robert Mitford came to be the Grand Master and Supreme Commander of the Templar Knights. The Templar Knights was a small but very powerful group of men with links to the FBI, the CIA, and other intelligence communities, including Cuban exiles. Membership of the Templar Knights was hereditary, with very strict selection criteria. It was an extreme right wing organization feared by politicians in the know. Its specialty was false flag activities including assassinations.

Robert was told to initiate plans to assassinate Nixon politically if Nixon were to renege on the long-standing agreements with Chiang Kai-shek of Taiwan and other allies in East Asia and the Pacific Rim. It was no small matter, as the reputation of the US with all its allies along the Pacific

Rim and beyond was at stake. MacDonald Douglas, Lockheed, and other players within the Military Industrial Complex[1] were supportive of this initiative. Armament sales to Taiwan were worth more than US$10 billion a year.

Nick had been given a free hand to do his magic. There was only one caveat; he must not be linked to the Military Industrial Complex or the China Lobby. After all, these were patriotic corporations and national organizations and did not get involved in plots.

Robert was to communicate with Nick only by way of a safety drop. No electronic means of communication was allowed or to be used. They were all open to eavesdropping by a multitude of organizations, not least the security agencies such as the FBI and the CIA. Normally, the CIA was not supposed to spy on US citizens. Its remit since its formation during and after the Second World War was to conduct espionage and counter-intelligence activities overseas. However, it had been hijacked by right wing anti-communist zealots. Surveillance of US citizens, although illegal, was thus commonplace. Anyway the issue under discussion was too delicate to expose it to even the slightest possibility of a leak.

'All Americans are brought up to believe in the high principles of freedom, honesty and liberty and equality, the fundamental ethos of our country. The general public fear being spied upon. If it can be demonstrated that Nixon is mounting widespread eavesdropping operations, we will have the entire country behind the call for his removal. We have to make use of the psyche of the normal American Joe Public', plotted Nick with a huge grin.

'The first steps would involve looking for scandalous material. The most common would be illicit affairs with women – the proverbial 'honey trap' to tempt the unsuspecting. This would be followed closely by a review of tax and financial affairs. It is said that Edgar Hoover retained his power by having files on the secrets of ALL United States notables. If this does not work then other false flag activities could be resorted to. If you throw enough mud on someone, some of it will stick,' chuckled Nick.

'Unfortunately, Nixon cannot be trapped on the issue of women or dodgy financial arrangements,' interjected Robert who had the scandals of all Washington notables on his extensive files.

'We have to be a great deal more subtle with him. We need to make use of his known weaknesses – tendency to delegate, fondness for secrecy, lax security but a sense of paranoia of the liberal left. He has been plagued by them throughout his whole political career. In that sense it is possible and relatively easy to blind-side him. He will be on the constant lookout for attacks from the left rather than from the right. We can use the campaign for re-election for a second term as the backdrop,' said Nick with his characteristic enthusiasm.

'A false flag action, such as a break in, has to be initiated. Such activities have to be repeated until one of them sticks. The arrest can be engineered with a trail of incriminating evidence. The advantage of such a scheme is that it will NOT be linked to the new China policy. If simultaneously a high principled question can be raised by the media, then the liberal left will run with the ball until a touchdown is achieved,' said Nick, pleased with his choice of metaphor from American football of which he was great fan.

'For our purpose, a touchdown is the effective destruction of Nixon's political life and a warning to all other potential turncoats. That is better than merely killing him physically. He would feel more pain being dragged through the mud. In any case, there have been three recent physical assassinations – JFK, Robert Kennedy and Martin Luther King Jr. Physical assassination is therefore out of the question. In a manner of speaking, a political assassination on the question of accountability of the President may have the added effect of uniting the country, something the United States sorely needs at this hour.

'Who are the people who would campaign for a Nixon presidential re-election? They are made up of a) the idealistic, b) cronies-on-the-make, and c) the in-crowd. These are the mindless dyed-in-the-wool Nixon loyalists who are in charge of the campaign for his re-election,' reflected Nick, answering his own question.

'I say that we should concentrate on cronies-on-the-make to set the trap and then we can depend on the idealists and the left wing press to carry the ball over for a touchdown. The "story" of the trap has to be acceptable and supported by both parties. I would suggest using "the abuse of power" gambit. It will have near-universal support. Everyone in the country is instinctively fearful of Big Brother's interferences and interventions in his life. Most of the population have heard of if not read the novel 1984[2]. If we can engender an "abuse of power" narrative, it would more or less be a guarantee of success. I would suggest that once we have decided on the basic idea of the trap, the actual workings can be improvised. I propose a break in to a high profile target such as the offices of the Democratic National Committee at Watergate,' suggested Robert warming to the plot.

'It may be necessary for several break ins for the conspirators, including our double agent, to be caught. Once the trap has been sprung, it would be a matter of drip-feeding the media with nuggets of information that will generate fear and outcry. I want the accusation against the Nixon team to be imprinted on the national psyche. The media must be fed with lots of misleading details to get journalists off the scent. We have to insinuate one of our people into CREEP, the Committee to Re-elect the President. This is the more sinister acronym instead of the official CRP. Our mole can propose activities that will lead to an arrest. If we plant incriminating evidence among the conspirators that lead to the White House, then it is a question of getting a young idealistic journalist hack to investigate and report the story. Oh, how I love to see all this happen. Thus we need a) someone to inform us of developments; b) someone to feed information to the press; and finally c) someone within the White House who will deliver the coup *de grâce*,' said Robert as he pressed on with his plans and getting quite excited.

'Of course all our players will have the proper back-up, but will be ignorant of one another. I propose that we use the "cell" model. Each cell will be under the control of a controller who knows exactly who its members are. However, knowledge of the cell's activities will be on a strict "need-to-know" basis. Each cell member will be unaware of the activities of the other cells. Thus, even if a cell leaks, the systematic cut-outs will prevent the activities of the project being leaked. The cell is the basic unit of conspiratorial organizations. We have to fight fire with fire,' said Nick pleased with his contributions.

'The person to infiltrate CREEP, ideally, has to be a young disillusioned Vietnam veteran, or someone who vehemently detests Nixon but who can also feign loyalty and tell a good story. We need someone to suggest plausible tactics that will lead to arrests pointing to the White House,' continued Robert.

'The White House mole ideally is a suitably qualified lawyer. There are many, who are on the make, who would grab at the chance. They do not even have to be aware of the plot in the beginning. When the heat gets to them, they will start squealing to protect their arse,' elaborated Robert.

'Finally, – the feeder of information – a person disillusioned with one of our multitude of investigative agencies and an enemy of Nixon, for whatever reason, would be suitable. I would suggest the FBI. I am sure that with his years of listening to our politicians, Edgar Hoover can find just the person we need,' said Nick with cunning in his voice.

'I understand that Holmberg is not happy. Perhaps I could sound him out tactfully,' Robert ventured.

Robert, having listened carefully to Nick's contributions on security measures, spoke again, 'It is my understanding that you want this to be launched when campaigning for the presidential election starts in earnest. We shall use the safety drop at the club house to make contact. I shall use locker number 46 and invisible ink with messages written on nondescript invoices of local shops.

'I agree fully with you that money is the language best understood by the cronies-on-the-make. The beautiful thing is that most of the money shall come from the campaign slush funds that all candidates have. I will persuade one of our major corporations to transfer $500,000 in the first instance to Nixon's re-election campaign fund.

'I shall use my own cut-outs to instruct those faggots. For the plan to work, the arrest has to be of high enough profile to be reported in the papers. We must leave a trail for the intrepid to follow. The trail must not be too easy as otherwise someone may smell a rat. Nixon has so many enemies that I can mount a false flag action within forty-eight hours of receiving a "go" signal,' said Robert smugly.

'I shall start activating my contacts this evening. By next week we will have a plan at the ready. It is fairly well known that both sides use money-laundering to make the sources of their slush fund untraceable. Monies for the operation can be given to the slush fund under the care of Maurice Stans. I have heard that the rascal is still using the old methods of laundering money in Mexico to make the sources of the funds untraceable. It is as if he is unaware that Nixon has passed the Federal Election Campaign (FEC) Act banning such practices. It must be a case of old dogs don't learn new tricks. I shall run a check on that.

'If what is being said is true then that makes life easier. I shall arrange for a money trail when money is spent on the cronies-on-the-make. I know several of them and it is easy to provide them with access to the Campaign to Re-elect President Nixon, CRP for short, and CREEP to us. We will leak it to the media who will love to propagate it.

'We should start referring to CRP as CREEP. It has the ring of the dank nastiness that the media have created around Nixon. Much should be made of the media to refer to President Nixon as "Tricky Dickie". With Tricky Dickie and CREEP, we have two sinister sound bites that will horrify and terrify the electorate. The media would love it and will propagate the idea of a sinister and nasty Nixon. We will have to dig the dirt for the events of the 1950s such as the Hiss indictment in which Nixon played such a crucial role. He has made so many enemies among the liberal press barons, many of whom have never forgiven him for showing them to be wrong. It is important that we revive all the old anti-Nixon propaganda to prepare the population and instill in their minds that Nixon is the nasty piece of work that he is generally known to be.

'We should stir up and remind the liberal press of the infamous Alger Hiss trial of the early 1950s when Nixon made his name. We must link Nixon with his past anti-liberal and anti-communist activities. This is sure to get the liberal free press going. We have to build a united front of the liberal left in order to defeat him,' concluded Robert.

The two players finished their round of golf and went back to the club house, where they each had the customary shower. On this occasion they skipped the Swedish massage that was on offer and went their separate ways.

CHAPTER 4 - THE NIXON PLAN

It was the summer of 1971 and Henry Kissinger had just returned from his clandestine trip to China. Nixon summoned and met with his National Security Council Advisor that evening. Nixon started by recalling parts of his first inaugural speech made in 1969:

'Forces now are converging that make possible, for the first time, the hope that many of man's deepest aspirations can at last be realized. The spiraling pace of change allows us to contemplate, within our own lifetime, advances that once would have taken centuries.

'To the crisis of the spirit, we need an answer of the spirit.

'To find that answer, we need only look within ourselves.

'The peace we seek to win is not victory over any other people, but the peace that comes with healing in its wings; with compassion for those who have suffered; with understanding for those who have opposed us; with the opportunity for all the peoples of this earth to choose their own destiny.

'I wonder how many people caught the true meanings of my words,' he mused. 'Henry, do you know why I chose you?' he asked rhetorically. Feeling generous, he continued, 'I was most impressed by your writings on geopolitics, in particular your book Nuclear Weapons and Foreign Policy [1]. When I read it, I knew that you were the one person who thinks like me.'

Nixon went on to give an account of how he saw the changing world and what needed to be done. He was prone to long soliloquies.

'America is no longer as strong as she was after the Second World War. We made several mistakes. The Korean War[2] was a mistake. So is the Vietnam War. We have no bloody business to be there. The damned Democrats and their falling dominoes; they are the cause of all our problems. Sharp divisions within our great country have been caused by the Vietnam War. Don't listen to the motherfucking four-starred generals. The morale among our ground troops is at rock bottom. I know because I have ears among them. It seems like we have to have our people everywhere.

'Other than you, I don't trust anyone,' Nixon felt he had to be generous to bond with Henry. In truth he did not trust Henry either. He thought that Kissinger[3] was a power-hungry opportunist with an eye on the money and an egotist. He could make use of the latter quality to get him to work on the China project. He was also aware of Henry's fondness for the opposite sex which was an obvious weakness. However, Kissinger's mastery of geopolitics and diplomacy was a strength that Nixon and America could ill-afford to pass over just because of a presumed weakness for the opposite sex.

'Most of the young are against an unwinnable war of adventure thousands of miles from our shores. The only people who have benefitted are the large corporations that make up what Ike, bless his soul, called the Military Industrial Complex.

'It is a mistake to think that the Soviets and Red China would make up an indivisible and unassailable bloc. There has been a shooting war between the Soviets and the Red Chinese and there are now some twenty-seven divisions[4] of the Soviet army across the Chinese border.

'This change in geopolitics gives us a unique opportunity to play the China card to extricate us from the Vietnamese quagmire that we have inherited from the Democrats. I want Peace with Honour. There can be no other way, if the United States were to get out of Vietnam holding its head high and maintain its position as the leader of the free world. This is a non-negotiable position.

'What I want to do is politically dangerous and if badly timed could mean political suicide for me. But the country is in mortal danger and I am therefore prepared to take the risks. You are aware of my aim to reach a rapprochement with China and are helping me to see it through.

'The Red Chinese want to be the revolutionary leaders of the world. But they are also fearful of upsetting the Soviets. What they say publicly is all so much bluster.

'I am sure that the Chinese leaders are also aware that peasants cannot fight and win a war against a modern nuclear power. Mao may rant and rave about paper tigers. It is good for morale, but not an effective weapon against nuclear annihilation. The Chinese are working at breakneck speed to build up their nuclear arsenal. I do not want a fight with them.

'The Korean War was an aberration, a failure in diplomacy. It had been said that Stalin lured the Chinese into a fight with us in order to weaken both adversaries. It was much like our ploy in the Second World War for the two totalitarian states, Germany and the Soviet Union to mutually exhaust each other. Our mistake was that we underestimated the resilience of the Soviet army. That was why they got to Berlin before us.

'The Chinese will maintain that they cannot speak for the Vietnamese people. China is an old country, the country of Sunzi. I have been reading Sunzi and learning to think along the lines recommended by him. We can play the three cornered game of Three Kingdoms. We do not have to get the Chinese to put pressure on the Vietnamese. As long as the Reds know that our aim is to pull out of Vietnam, their actions and decisions will be influenced and modified by that knowledge. This is particularly true if we maintain our secret channel with the Reds and cultivate a degree of trust, you might say.

'Once the Vietnamese become aware of our contact with Mao's China, they will harbour suspicions of the true nature of China's support. That will divide the Red camp even further. Henry, you are my Zhuge Liang.' Nixon loved to show off his erudition in classical Chinese literature.

'By the way, are Warsaw, Ottawa and Pakistan secure?' Nixon threw a question at Kissinger which was not answered as Kissinger thought it beneath him to answer such a patronizing question about the secret channels to China. Henry was willing to put up with Nixon's famed soliloquies on the basis that if Nixon was talking to him, then he was not talking with any other potential rival.

'I want you to make sure that there is no leak of our plans until we are ready to make the announcement, ' continued Nixon.

'The American people love drama and theatre. They have been involved in a love-hate relationship with China, ever since the days of Pearl S Buck[5]. Our missionaries have built schools and universities there. You could say that the last twenty years have been years of unrequited love. Our change in foreign policy direction will be a drama that will do the American people proud. I will give the American people a theatrical gift they won't forget. It will catch their imagination. Something they will not forget for a very long time. It should also ensure my re-election in November 1972. That is the beauty of this strategy. Killing several birds with just a single stone.

'There will be opposition. I can see it coming from the China Lobby, the right wing Republicans and their scribes – people such as Pat Buchanan and William Buckley.

'The China Lobby may be filled with yesterday's men fighting yesterday's wars. But they are extremely well connected. I should know from the McCarthy days when I was beavering away as a political advisor. They can be very nasty and vicious, those sons of bitches. I know because I used to work within their midst.

'The corporations making up the Military Industrial Complex will feel threatened by our aim to pull out of Vietnam. They are profiting billions of greenbacks even though the country is going bankrupt. They don't care, but I do.

'To placate them, we will have to have something up our sleeves in the language that they understand which CASH is. I shall stuff their mouths with cash from tax cuts and other cash goodies. My reputation as an anti-communist will ensure that the right-of-centre elements and the big corporations be placated. This is one of the reasons why I have put up with the vilifications by the liberal left all these years.

'Oh, remind me to share my thinking about the dollar and gold. The frogs across the pond are stirring up trouble on that front, trying to withdraw their gold reserves.' Nixon was referring to the initiative led by de Gaulle of France to demand gold[6] in exchange for the mass of US dollars held in reserve by France. 'I am minded to break the linkage between the dollar and gold. We don't have enough gold in Fort Knox to repay our debts. If I pass a law to break the link between the dollar and gold and create the world's first ever fait reserve currency, the frogs may scream as the dollar floats, but we would be out of a crisis in a thrice. Also it will guarantee several decades of prosperity for Americans.

'I owe that one to John,' referring to the scheme of his Democrat Secretary of the Treasury. 'We must make use of the power inherent in the greenbacks being the world's reserve currency. Nobody will notice the difference. It also means that all we have to do is to print more dollars when more money is required. This is an advantage that comes from being the most powerful country of the Free World.

'While I have my doubts about the domino theory, it has served as an excellent propaganda ploy to rein in our allies around the Pacific Rim. However, I do believe in the containment of the Soviets and China. If we can accentuate the division between the Soviets and the Chinese, it will make our tasks easier and the next world war less likely, and usher in decades of world peace. This is the beauty of the theory of triangulation among three powers in the world.

'It was ingenious of Churchill and Roosevelt to have the Soviets and the Nazis battle it out. We moved only when both were exhausted. Thereafter, America displaced Great Britain as the global power of the Free World.

'Of course we have to let the Brits believe that they are still a major power despite the fact that they still owe us billions in Lend-Lease Loans[7] that will take them years to repay. There is nothing to gain to rid the Brits of their self-deception as a great power. We must allow them to "punch above their weight" as long as they pay us what they owe and acknowledge allegiance to Uncle Sam.

'However, I do not see that all our allies will see things our way. After all we have blackballed the Red Chinese for over twenty years, and it is hard for our allies to see the sense of our proposals. You can bet that there will be protests in Taiwan, Japan, and South Korea.

'The Philippines, Indonesia, Singapore, and Malaysia may be easier to placate. They all have historical ties with European masters. We also have to think about the feelings of our Anglo-Saxon allies in Australia, New Zealand, and Canada. Of course we must not forget Britain, our beachhead in Europe.

'I would so much like to let Teddy Heath in on our act, but I am concerned about leaks emanating from Britain. Their Foreign and Commonwealth Office is worse than a colander.

'Then there are the Soviets. I need to keep them sweet, without causing too much concern to the Chinks.'

'Sir, I could propose to the Chinese that we would keep them informed of developments with the Soviets. We can even give them some of our intelligence material on the Soviet Union to reassure them of our good faith.' Kissinger was used to having to sit in on these long monologues, interjecting only with his own Machiavellian schemes. He was a shrewd political player himself.

Nixon gave Kissinger a big slap on his back, 'Henry, I would not want to buy a second-hand car from you. That is a great idea. Let us go for it. But please do not let the cunts at Foggy Bottom get wind of this. I don't trust them one bit.'

'Don't worry, boss. Poor William Rogers, your eminent Secretary of State is completely in the dark. So much so that he has nominated one of his flunkies to sit in at the meetings of the National Security Council (NSC). I saw the poor bugger taking down notes and photo-copying position papers assiduously the other day. The poor bugger does not know that I have turned the NSC into a front, a talking shop of no consequence. Nothing of actual major consequence is discussed there.' Kissinger feinting humility, drone on in his heavy guttural German Jewish accent.

'Tell me about your trip to China,' encouraged Nixon.

'Well, as instructed by you, it was an elaborate case of smoke and mirrors. I had sent a message through Ambassador Agha Hilaly, our Pakistan channel to the Chinese, giving them the message that I would like to discuss matters of mutual interest. That was done in early April after our table tennis team's visit to Red China.' Henry Kissinger started to relate his account.

'Oh Henry, although we are used to referring to the Chinese as the Reds, we must be careful not to use those words. Soon we will have to refer them as the People's Republic of China. The Chinese are nitpickers. I don't want a small matter like that to jeopardize my initiative,' interjected Nixon. Nixon had used the words 'People's Republic of China', for the first time at a banquet given in his honour in Rumania in the autumn of 1970.

'The Pakistanis are very aware of the highly sensitive nature of their work for us. Agha Hilaly personally writes down our messages, reads them to Yahya Khan, the Prime Minister who then writes down his own version to be read personally to the Chinese, usually Premier Zhou. Both handwritten notes are destroyed after use. The system is slow but is fool proof against leaks.

'I asked the Chinese to observe the utmost secrecy for your first ever visit, although it will be announced when it is over. We need that arrangement just in case no agreement can be arrived at. I do not want any last minute hitch to trouble your trip. The Chinese agreed to our request without any fuss. This is a good indication that they want a rapprochement as much as we do. It does no harm to our negotiating position to know that.' Henry Kissinger was warming up to his account. It was good not to have to listen to his boss, Nixon.

'On April 27, 1971, Hilaly handed me the answer from the Chinese. The trip is on, with agreement to all our conditions for secrecy.

'For discussion on the trip, I had asked to meet with Premier Zhou. Ambassador Farland was flown to California from Pakistan. We flew from there to Rawalpindi. Ambassador Farland told a huge whopper to the press that I had a tummy bug and had to rest at the hill-station. That was the excuse we used to give me the time to fly to China, meet with Zhou and return to Pakistan.

'In my meeting with Zhou at the Great Hall of the People, I was very frank with the Chinese. We want to extricate from Vietnam. They said that Taiwan is the main issue for them. I indicated to them that I was aware of the significance of holding the talks at the Fujian Room of the Great Hall as Fujian is directly opposite to Taiwan. They wanted a timetable of complete US withdrawal from Taiwan. I told them that it was politically impossible to do that. As a sop I agreed to their formula that there is only one China. I had no problem with that as Chiang in Taiwan says that too. It was also agreed that the US would eventually withdraw from Taiwan, but no timing was specified.

'As expected, the Chinese refused to co-operate on Vietnam. Their position is that they cannot tell the North Vietnamese what to do. As previously agreed by you, I pretended to argue the point but gave way as a sign of our willingness to make concessions. Anyway, our objective was to let them know of our intention as that would influence their approach and decision-making process. I also passed on your instructions that no other Americans should be invited to visit China before your trip, especially politicians from the Democratic Party.' Kissinger was slyly letting out that he was out-smarting the Chinese.

'From my reading of the public pronouncements and the diplomatic cables, although our allies have expressed their objections vehemently in public, I think there will be no major problems from them. Anyway, they do realize that they depend on our patronage. As a precaution, I did arrange for our representatives to visit all the hot locations to calm their nerves.

'I obtained agreement that you will be invited to visit China in February 1972. I insisted on an invitation, as I do not wish it be said that we are the supplicants. They were vague about whether you would meet with Mao. I insisted on a meeting, as, without a meeting, the impression may be conveyed that your trip has failed. I am afraid I could not obtain a firm yes. It is a risk, but I am confident that the Chinese, because they want this rapprochement as much as we do, but for different reasons, will comply. The final communique[8] has also not been settled. The proposed formula is that each side would state its respective position i.e. the differences and then the areas of agreement. This was insisted upon by Zhou in order that the final communique is to be meaningful; instead of a communique of bland diplomatic language. I have no problems with the formula. The actual wording will be thrashed out in Shanghai[8] during your visit. It is my reading that they are playing hardball mind games with us,' concluded Kissinger, summing up the gist of his clandestine trip to China.

CHAPTER 5 - NIXON VISITS CHINA

On February 19, 1972 Nixon with Kissinger, Pat Nixon and staff flew to Hawaii on route to China[1].

It was a cold day, but Nixon was in high spirits. This was despite there being several issues that had not been resolved. Foremost was the meeting with Mao; would he or would he not meet Mao? Failure to meet Mao could be construed as a snub and a failure on his part. He had brought with him some hundred correspondents for newspapers and television. Advanced parties had been out to China to ensure that there was satellite communication and to look out for photo opportunity spots. The Chinese had been puzzled by the great emphasis on the media. They had initially allocated ten correspondents and the number had been negotiated to above a hundred technical staff.

Some senior media executives had to have their places assigned as technical staff and had to lug equipment as the price for going to China with Nixon, there being such a rush to be part of the historic party.

There was also the issue of the final communique. It was important that Nixon had something concrete to show for the trip. The document should sum up the current situation as each party saw it and how to progress forward.

What would China hold? What were the people like? Would they be hostile or friendly? These were the questions high on the minds of the correspondents. They were in an optimistic frame of mind as the Chinese had proven to be friendly and co-operative to the advance parties.

Nixon was handed a thick briefing book with the CIA emblem in the front. He jokingly laughed and said that he could be arrested in China for having such a contraband book.

In Nixon's mind this trip to China had two purposes: one to change the world balance of power in favour of peace on America's terms; and second to garner votes for his re-election. The Americans had a love-hate relation with China since the first novels by Pearl S Buck at the turn of the century. These past twenty odd years had been like a prolonged period of unrequited love. However, if Nixon could show the American people on prime time TV that he had built a bridge to China he would be assured of their vote and would be on to a winner. This was why he had instructed Kissinger during the negotiation for this trip to seek agreement by the Chinese not to talk to his Democratic opponents or to agree to any visits by them. This was also why the Americans had negotiated the setting up of a satellite dish and some hundred TV broadcasting staff. Nixon was disappointed by the lack of a welcoming crowd at his arrival at Shanghai and then in Beijing. They would have been such great photo opportunities. Imagine an American President being welcomed by a crowd of Chinese. However, the Chinese, with their sense of history and a long memory, while prepared to be hospitable, were not prepared to overlook past historical slights such as the signs in Shanghai that said 'Chinese and dogs are not allowed[2]'. It would also have been most inappropriate to pretend that everything was hunky dory on this first visit.

When Nixon's plane, the *Spirit of 76* (Air Force One until Nixon declared that it should be renamed) landed in Beijing, his agents informed him that as Premier Zhou Enlai was wearing an overcoat, he should do the same rather than brave the cold northern winds. As Nixon stepped off the portable stairs leading from the *Spirit of 76,* he stuck his hand out to shake that of the Chinese Premier. Nixon was making sure that the snub by John Foster Dulles[3] to refuse to shake Zhou's hand when they met in 1954 in Geneva was erased by his conscious gesture. By so doing, Nixon demonstrated his sensitivity and sense of history. He had deeply regretted the Dulles slight on the Chinese and wanted to make amends.

In their drive from the airport, Zhou said to Nixon, 'Your handshake came over the vastest ocean in the world – twenty-five years of no communication.' Nixon was pleased with the diplomatic feather in his cap. His good grace was reported very favourably by the press.

The motorcade drove through Tiananmen Square to the west of the city to the special Diaoyutai State Guesthouse reserved for visiting foreign heads of state and dignitaries. The Diaoyutai complex was built in 1959 to celebrate the tenth anniversary of the founding of the People's Republic. Kim Il Sung, Nikita Khrushchev and Ché Guevara had all preceded Nixon in being housed within the compound. It was rumoured that Prince Sihanouk[4] of Cambodia had recently moved out of the villa that was to house Nixon and his entourage.

The rooms were filled with oversized sofas and settees, each with its own antimacassar. Nixon and Zhou Enlai sat side by side on a sofa while the rest of their respective entourages sat in a semi-circle, sipping tea politely and listening to the conversation. Nixon had agreed to dispense with American interpreters and used the Chinese ones.

Nixon, the consummate politician, was showing signs of agitation that there had been no word that he would meet with Chairman Mao. It must happen, otherwise his fellow Americans at home would consider that a snub. Kissinger was unable to give him any assurance that a meeting had been arranged. The meeting would also have historic significance. Nixon loved to view his projects within their historical context, and building a bridge to China had been his ambition for many years. He felt very emotional now that his long-held passion was bearing fruit.

Nixon had hardly settled at his quarters, when word came that Mao would like to meet with him. The message was delivered by Zhou himself. It was obvious that Mao was just as excited to meet the head honcho of the US imperialists. Nixon, Kissinger, and his aide were around but William Rogers the Secretary of State had stepped out and could not be found.

The Chinese, ever sensitive to the check and balance of the United States political system, had housed the White House staff some distance away from those of the Foggy Bottom.

This was a probable reason why William Rogers was not to be readily found for the meeting with Mao.

Making a choice between upsetting Rogers and missing an appointment with Mao was a no brainer. They bundled themselves like excited schoolboys into the 'Red Flag' state limousine and made their way south to Mao's quarters in Zhongnanhai, the exclusive residential compound for Mao and other top members of the Chinese Communist Party. In order to placate William Rogers and to avoid a public fallout, Winston Lord, Kissinger's aide, was cropped out of the official photograph recording Nixon's meeting with Mao.

The meeting with Mao, although an excellent photo opportunity, was actually not very substantive in political terms. Mao seemed to skirt around any issues raised by Nixon in favour of a general discussion of philosophical matters. It looked as if the nitty-gritty of the trip had to be resolved with Premier Zhou. Was this a ploy by the Chinese in order to have a way to renege on matters agreed?

Nixon was not overly concerned, as he wanted the propaganda kudos associated with being the first American President to visit the People's Republic of China. It had latterly been made known that Mao had recently been ill but had insisted on meeting with Nixon, so excited was he at the prospect of meeting with the President.

CHAPTER 6 - PREPARING THE TRAP

Nixon had returned from his very successful trip to China. His trip had caught the imagination of the majority of Americans and won their support. At the same time it had caught his Democratic Party opponents completely unawares. The popularity of the China initiative had been confirmed by initial polls. The polls were beginning to turn in Nixon's favour, having reached a nadir after the botched invasion of Cambodia and the fatal shootings at Kent State University.

Nixon began to focus his attention on the coming re-election campaign that was to take place in November 1972, less than a year away. The Committee to Re-elect the President (CRP), although formed in the Spring of 1971 with offices at 1701 Pennsylvania Avenue, had remained dormant.

Daniel Ellsberg's leaking of the Pentagon Papers[1] to *The New York Times* seemed initially to show that the Kennedys were not so clean after all. It had also revealed that President Johnson had in fact 'manufactured' the Gulf of Tonkin Incident that led to the escalation of the Vietnam War. Nixon had initially thought that the leaks were politically to his advantage.

However, Nixon's assessment of the scandal was soon to change when the size and nature of the leaks began to embarrass the United States government. The leaks had turned into a flood when not only *The New York Times*, but

The Washington Post, *The Boston Globe* and the *Chicago Sun-Times* were publishing sensitive leaked documents. Nixon decided that the leaks were detrimental to the proper functioning of the United States government. After all, he had solemnly sworn on his family Bible at his first inauguration to defend the United States which meant its government, a task that Nixon took very seriously.

Nixon summoned his inner circle of lieutenants – Bob Haldeman, John Ehrlichman, Charles Colson and Jeb Magruder – to a meeting at his office at the Executive Office Building (EOB)[2] instead of the Oval Office. Nixon had felt that the Oval Office was too formal and had preferred to work in the office at the EOB. He had instructed them on no account to give interviews to the media on the Pentagon Papers and also to re-activate the Committee to Re-elect the President in preparation for the re-election campaign. 'I do not want anyone to give briefings to the press about the Pentagon Papers. Although I initially thought that the leaks would be to our political advantage, they are now embarrassing to the government of the United States and making it difficult for it to function properly.

'Furthermore I think it is time we brought CRP out of its mothball. With Senator Teddy Kennedy out of the running after Chappaquiddick[3] I feel fairly comfortable with the domestic political situation. It would be better if Senator George McGovern is nominated to be our opponent. While I am delegating you all to run my re-election campaign so that I can concentrate on foreign affairs, we must not be complacent and let the Democrats steal the election.'

Nixon had shown a disdain for domestic politics that bordered on the negligent. Thus, while he paid all his attention on his foreign policy initiatives, he had a 'couldn't be bothered' attitude when it came to domestic affairs. He was quietly confident that he had done enough during his first term to ensure that he would win comfortably at the re-election. He was therefore quite happy to delegate the running of his re-election campaign to his lieutenants while he worked on the next part of his grand foreign policy design, which was the SALT summit in Moscow, another first for an American president. While he was aware that the political right might not be happy with his approaches to China and the Soviet Union, he was rather confident that his policy of Peace with Honour would pacify the right wingers. He had concluded that his main threat came from the left; the media hysteria over Watergate soon confirmed his hunch.

Robert Mitford had little difficulty in getting his operatives into the White House. It was said that he was even able to get a person into Kissinger's entourage. The China Lobby knew that Kissinger had been to China. They even had a copy of the secret cable that Kissinger had sent Nixon. Although portrayed as paranoiac, Nixon would delegate tasks dealing with domestic politics to Bob Haldeman or John Ehrlichman. Ehrlichman was soon to be promoted to be the Domestic Policy Chief. It was a position of great power and responsibility. Nixon was more concerned with foreign affairs, his first love, rather than domestic politics. This was despite his belief that John Kennedy stole the election in 1960 as he had lost by only 100,000 votes. While he was aware that the policy of withdraw from Vietnam and his foreign policy initiatives with China and the Soviet Union would upset the members of the Military Industrial Complex, he thought he could pacify them with the tax cuts and other cash goodies in the pipeline. Furthermore, he had always fought for the overall interests of the United States of America. He had calculated that he had enough support among the Republicans to more than neutralize his extreme right wing opponents. He was more concerned with attacks from the left, especially from Teddy Kennedy who might just steal his second term. However, after Chappaquiddick, he knew that Teddy Kennedy would be a spent force. His enemies in the China Lobby had read him correctly.

Robert Mitford had got his agents to instigate the leaking of the Pentagon Papers to *The New York Times i*n order to test the water and also to wrong-foot Nixon.

When Daniel Ellsberg, a disillusioned Vietnam veteran, was identified as the source of the leak of the Pentagon Papers from the Brookings Institute, a liberal think-tank, Nixon swore to get his man. He needed to make an example of Ellsberg so that any person tempted to leak government papers would be put off by the draconian consequences. It was not clear who had suggested the formation of the White House Intelligence Unit, known also as the 'plumbers', to prevent leaks.

Nixon's relaxed attitude seemed to have filtered down the ranks. There were no formal security checks. In a word, it was shambolic, as predicted by the China Lobby conspirators. Thus Howard Hunt, Gordon Liddy, and Jerome 'Nuts' Lieberman were recruited into the team of 'plumbers'. The 'plumbers' was the White House response to the lack of cooperation against leaks by both the intelligence services, the Federal Bureau of Investigations and the Central Intelligence Agency. It was a small step then to get the 'plumbers' to work for the Committee to Re-elect the President, when the campaign began in earnest, and the White House became short of staff.

Howard Hunt had glowing references. He was involved in implementing the Marshall Plan in post-war Europe, often working against the agents of the Soviet Union. He was a cold warrior, having worked for the Central Intelligence Agency in Vienna, Madrid, Tokyo, Mexico and Uruguay before retiring to form his own security consultancy. He had also known some success as a writer of thrillers with right wing themes. He used to boast that he was a spy for the United States government, having worked for both the Eisenhower and the Kennedy administrations with regard to the Bay of Pigs project. He therefore had intimate links with anti-communists and anti-Castro Cubans.

Gordon Liddy was a friend of Charles Chuck Colson, a loyal White House lawyer. Colson had been with the Green Berets and was notorious for having on his wall the sign 'If you've got 'em by the balls the hearts and minds will follow.' Gordon Liddy had worked for the FBI and was reputed to have caught the eye of Edgar Hoover, the FBI director. Liddy was also a friend of Egil Krogh who worked as John Ehrlichman's deputy. Liddy was later (in the 1980s) to be associated with Timothy Leary, a Harvard psychologist of LSD fame. Nixon had referred to Timothy Leary as 'the most dangerous man in America.' Gordon Liddy was a Roman Catholic and had the reputation to be an anti-communist fanatic. He was very brave and his favourite party trick was to place his hand over a flame to show that he could withstand immense pain. His hands were often bandaged to cover the burn wounds that he had deliberately inflicted upon himself. He had also worked in the past with Howard Hunt.

Jerome 'Nuts' Lieberman was a shady character, having worked for both intelligence agencies in his chequered career. He had acquired the nick name 'Nuts' for making crazy over-the-top proposals to take out opponents of the United States. He was fearless and was reputed to have notched up more than fifty kills to his credit.

John Dean who was to become the youngest White House Special Counsel at the young age of thirty-one, was recruited by John Ehrlichman from an introduction by his deputy, Egil Krogh. John Dean was to replace Ehrlichman who had moved to be the Domestic Policy Chief. John Dean was an associate deputy attorney-general and had worked with John Mitchell the Attorney-General before Mitchell retired to take charge of CRP. John Dean soon made himself indispensable to the White House staff as he advised them on legal problems pertaining to conflict of interests.

James McCord was also recruited to CRP by Jeb Magruder, the young staffer who was nominally in charge of CRP in

John Mitchell's absence. McCord was soon to be promoted to be Magruder's deputy.

Thus Howard Hunt, Gordon Liddy, James McCord, Jerome 'Nuts' Lieberman and John Dean came to be among those recruited to the White House staff in preparation for the re-election campaign. Although Nixon did not have such problems, the distinction between enemies of the state and political enemies was less clear to his subordinates. 'Nuts' Lieberman would suggest fire-bombing the office of Dr Fielding who was Daniel Ellsberg's psychiatrist. Gordon Liddy, not to be outdone, had proposed buying a fire-engine to drive the 'plumbers' to Dr Fielding's office to raid the confidential files on Daniel Ellsberg during the fire. Gordon Liddy's proposal was overruled and a simple break in was authorized.

Howard Hunt and Gordon Liddy with their Cuban operatives were able to break into Dr Fielding's consulting rooms and removed Daniel Ellsberg's confidential medical records. The raid was widely reported, fulfilling the White House intention to bring the fear of God to any person tempted to leak government documents. No direct orders were issued from the White House. Those in authority believed they were carrying out Nixon's wishes. It was very much like the case of Thomas Becket and Henry the Second and his four knights, but without the murder.

The Daniel Ellsberg break in identified the 'plumbers' as an almost autonomous unit, able to embark on even the most lawless activities – just what was needed to trap Nixon.

Robert Mitford was able to report success of the first part of the operation to Nick Cato in a note delivered to locker 46 and written in invisible ink on the back of an innocent-looking invoice of a local hardware shop. Everything appeared to be in place to spring the trap when the presidential race commenced in earnest in a few months. That was March 1972.

A year before, in February 1971, Nixon made the fateful decision to reverse his earlier policy of dismantling President Johnson's taping system by installing his own. He had been convinced by Edgar Hoover who, quoting Sir Winston Churchill, had advised Nixon that the only reliable historical account of his presidency would be his own memoirs, and a secret taping system would help him to remember the key facts. The taping system was to be his downfall. Other presidents, including Franklin Roosevelt, had systems which were manually operated. Nixon's system was voice operated and therefore automatic. It was considered to be infallible and yet safe as only Nixon, Haldeman, Alexander Butterfield and a few Security Service personnel knew of the existence of the taping system.

CHAPTER 7 - SALT SUMMIT

May 26, 1972 was the first ever meeting of a United States President with his counterpart in Moscow. The Strategic Arms Limitation talks had begun earlier in 1969 during the first half of Nixon's first term, the meetings alternating between Helsinki and Vienna. It had been delayed over the issue of verification. The sticking point was that neither side was prepared to have its nuclear sites inspected by the other. Although a breakthrough had been reached in May 1971, it was nearly a year later that Nixon was to meet with Brezhnev in Moscow to sign the Strategic Arms Limitation Treaty.

By making the trip to Moscow Nixon was able to deliver to the world the first Strategic Arms Limitation Treaty. The United States, however, never ratified or signed the treaty. President Reagan unilaterally abolished the treaty in 1986. He then upped the ante for nuclear arms by declaring the Star Wars programme which was later reported to have bankrupted the Soviet Union and led to its break-up as a state. Nixon had been able to conduct the Strategic Arms Limitation talks despite his rapprochement with China. Many observers had predicted that Nixon's China policy would damage the United States' relations with the Soviet Union.

Nixon had read the Soviet Union's position correctly. He had figured that while the Soviet Union was concerned by his new friendly relations with China, it would do everything in its power to maintain a good working relation with the United States in order not to be isolated by China and the United States.

SALT had limited the number of nuclear warheads of both countries. Nixon was aware that the Soviet Union had embarked on an ambitious programme to develop more and better intercontinental ballistic missiles, especially the Multi-Re-entry Warhead Vehicles (MRV). The Strategic Arms Limitation Treaty was thus a way to delay the build-up of nuclear weapons by the Soviet Union. SALT was to lead to the Strategic Arms Reduction Talks (START) and the Nuclear Test Ban Treaties.

At SALT, it was agreed that each country would dissemble its nuclear warheads and limit the building of delivery systems. Nixon was able to realize what was at one time believed to be an impossible dream. He believed that he had brought about a safer world and that his grandchildren and others would be able to live without the sword of Damocles of nuclear destruction hanging above them.

.

CHAPTER 8 - SPRINGING THE TRAP

The first attempted break in to the offices of the Democratic National Committee coincided with Nixon's trip to Moscow. It was around late May, 1972. It was Jerome 'Nuts' Lieberman who first proposed the break in to the offices of the Democratic National Committee at Watergate. It was at a meeting of CRP held in the presence of John Mitchell, Jeb Magruder, Howard Hunt, Gordon Liddy, 'Nuts' Lieberman and James McCord. The White House 'plumbers' had become involved in the work of CRP.

'We need to know the plans of the Democratic Party. Information is power. Unless we know in advance the plans of our opponent, we will always be reacting when we need to be proactive. The Democratic National Committee has its headquarters in Watergate, a stone's throw from us. It would not take much to raid their offices,' proposed 'Nuts' Lieberman.

John Mitchell had judged that a raid with the removal of sensitive papers was too risky. Gordon proposed a scaled-down modification, 'Why don't we just place a few bugs in the offices? While there we could photograph any sensitive papers. This way, our intrusion would not be noticed and we can also listen to their plans.'

'Nuts' Lieberman and Liddy were soon able to persuade Howard Hunt and others of the merits of this plan. In the absence of Nixon, it was relatively easy to convince the likes of Jeb Magruder and John Mitchell of the merits of the break in to bug the offices. It was much less of a risk than a raid to steal sensitive papers.

It was on May 22, 1972 that the first attempt at a break in[1] took place. The raiders had rented an apartment numbered 419 at the Howard Johnson Motor Inn opposite the Watergate complex. Gordon Liddy broke an unwritten rule of the White House by getting James McCord involved in the break in attempt. The rule was that White House staff must never be implicated in legally dubious activities. Another new recruit, Al Baldwin was to be the lookout from the room at Howard Johnson's. The team consisted of James McCord, and the Cubans – Bernard Barker, Martinez, deDiego, Virgilio Gonzalez a locksmith, Renaldo Pico and Frank Sturgis who was also a United States citizen. The team was to have dinner at the Continental Room at Watergate. The plan was that after dinner, Howard Hunt and Gonzalez would stay back in the Continental Room and then make their way up to the offices of the Democratic National Committee, with Gonzalez picking the door locks so that the others could follow them.

However, the operation had to be abandoned as a security guard had seen Hunt and Gonzalez in the Continental Room at 10.30 pm, and both of them had to hide in a closet the entire night. They could not get into the stairwell as it was alarmed. The alarm was activated after 11:00 pm and they had missed the deadline. The operation was bizarrely organized as the booking for the dinner was made on paper with the letterhead of a Miami company that had Barker, one of the Cubans, as its director.

Anyway, the first attempt failed and planning then took place for the second attempt. This was even more bizarre in that all the raiders went in through the front door and signed the visitors' book. This attempt was partially successful in that bugs were planted into the offices of the Democratic National Committee, including that of its Chairman, Lawrence O'Brien. It soon became evident that only one of the bugs was working and the reception from the O'Brien bug was very poor.

A third attempt was proposed by 'Nuts' Lieberman. 'We have to replace the faulty bug as otherwise the operation would be a failure and we would be no further from whence we started.' By then, Magruder had bought replacement bugs at $30,000 each.

The third raid took place on the night of June 17, 1972. The day before, the two Cubans, Bernard Barker and Eugenio Martinez, checked into room 214 at the Watergate Hotel. They were followed by Sturgis and Gonzalez, another two Cubans, who checked into room 314. Since the second attempt Baldwin had a higher lookout (room 723) at the Howard Johnson Motor Inn. The view was better in that the new room was about three floors above and opposite the Democratic National Committee offices.

Before the third attempt, Liddy distributed cash to each of the five raiders in $100 bills. His idea was that each raider could use the money to bribe the police in the event that they were caught. How Liddy was able to get away with the assumption that the police were uniformly corrupt and why the money had consecutive serial numbers was never explained.

Neither was it certain who had slipped in the details of Howard Hunt's White House office into the address books of Bernard Barker and Eugenio Martinez.

It was then discovered that only four of the six walkie-talkies were working. The other two had flat batteries. Thus with Al Baldwin, the lookout based at Howard Johnson Motor Inn opposite the Watergate complex, and Liddy the leader of the operation, each having a walkie-talkie, there were only two walkie-talkies left for the five raiders. On the way to Watergate, Liddy was apprehended by traffic police for jumping amber traffic lights. When he finally arrived, Howard Hunt was already in room 214 ready to coordinate the raid.

The doors to the offices were picked and pieces of tape used to cover the locks so that the doors would close but not lock. Frank Willis, a junior security guard had first discovered that tapes had been placed over the locks to several of the doors. He took down the tapes and closed and locked the doors, but did not report the strange findings.

James McCord led the four Cubans into the Watergate complex. When it was discovered that the tapes had been removed, the raiders wanted to abort the break in. McCord spoke to Gordon Liddy, 'Hey Gordon, some damn fool has removed the tapes that were preventing the doors from locking. Although we can get Gonzalez to pick the locks again, it would take too long. I strongly suggest that the mission be aborted.' Gordon Liddy, however, insisted through the walkie-talkie that they proceeded with the raid. 'I insist that you guys proceed as planned. This is our third attempt and we must succeed. Get Gonzalez to pick the locks and you can tape them to facilitate your exit. It is all very quiet here.'

'Gordon, Gonzalez can pick the locks again, but it will mean at least another twenty minutes. I still think we should call this raid off.'

'James, I am telling you guys to proceed. We cannot countenance a third failed attempt at a simple break in. This is an order.'

The raiders had no choice but to proceed as ordered. Nobody would dare to countermand Liddy's orders. Gonzalez was able to pick the locks which were then taped to facilitate getting away. There was so much static interference to the walkie-talkies that Barker, the Cuban photographer, ordered that they be switched off as they were becoming too noisy and distracting. There was therefore no communication between the raiders and the lookout or Gordon Liddy, the leader of the operation.

Frank Willis was to rediscover that the tapes had been reapplied to several doors. Suspecting a break in, he phoned the police. It was 01:47 am, some fifty minutes from the time he first discovered that the door locks had been taped over. The burglars thus had plenty of time to get themselves into an irretrievable position. One of the inner doors had a lock that could not be picked. The Cubans had the not-so-bright idea of taking it down by unscrewing its hinges. A police car responded at 01:52 am. Although Baldwin could see the arrival of the police, he could not warn the raiders in the Watergate complex. Their walkie-talkies had been switched off.

Baldwin desperately called out to Gordon Liddy to inform him of the loss of communication and the arrival of police cars. 'Hi Gordon, we have a problem, I can see police cars arriving and yet our boys in Watergate are not responding. It looks as if their walkie-talkies have been switched off.'

'The police are entering the Watergate complex and in a couple of minutes would be at the offices of the Democratic National Committee. Our boys are still not responding,' Baldwin screamed down the walkie-talkie, getting more and more desperate. 'Oh dear, I can see the police apprehending our boys. I would suggest that you get away pronto if you do not wish to be arrested as well.'

When the police eventually got into the offices of the Democratic National Committee, they found the five raiders huddled together under a desk. They did not make a run for it nor did they put up a fight. The five gave the police their false identities which had been provided by Gordon Liddy:

Frank Carte (Bernard Barker)

Jene Valdez (Eugenio Martinez)

Raoul Godoy (Virgilio Gonzalez)

Edward Hamilton (Frank Sturgis)

Edward Matin (James McCord)

Howard Hunt and Gordon Liddy were just able to make their escape from rooms of the Watergate Hotel. The police had heard the chatter to their walkie-talkies and were able to trace them to the rooms at Watergate and also to room 723 at the Howard Johnson Motor Inn. Liddy and Hunt had left in such a hurry that much of the spare surveillance equipment were left in the rooms and recovered by the police.

Howard Hunt was to disappear for some months before surfacing to be indicted with rest of the raiders. This was after large sums of money, in the order of hundreds of thousand dollars, had been handed over to pay for his sick wife's medical treatment.

On Sunday, June 18, 1972, *The Washington Post* ran the banner headline 'Five held in Plot to bug Democratic Offices'. The headline was placed at the bottom of page one. The paper reported that a team of burglars had been arrested inside the Watergate offices of the Democratic National Committee in Washington DC. The White House was implicated by the presence of James McCord and also by the references to Howard Hunt's address at the White House. In fact, Howard Hunt had ceased working at the White House at the time of the arrest.

Thus the trap was sprung at the third attempt to raid the Watergate offices of the Democratic Party. The rest of the plot was relatively easy to enact. The deep cover source revealed by *The Washington Post* in September 1972 as

'Deep Throat' was able to provide just the right amount of juicy tit-bits and at the right moment to keep the story alive. Bob Woodward and Carl Bernstein were the two intrepid journalists to uncover the Watergate cover-up.

When Nixon heard about the raid he was apoplectic with anger, and berated the 'plumbers'. 'There was no reason for the raid. We are already more than twenty-six points ahead of Senator George McGovern. What were you guys thinking of?'

His campaign managers, feeling foolish and sorry, tried to placate Nixon by playing down the significance of the arrests. They convinced him that the Watergate break in to the headquarters of the Democratic National Committee in circumstances that were almost hilarious would be considered as a tit-for-tat raid. After all, the Nixon headquarters in Phoenix had been burnt down. Significantly, they never mentioned that Howard Hunt's details were in the address books nor that money carried by the raiders had consecutive serial numbers traceable to CRP and hence to the White House. Nixon reluctantly accepted their arguments that nothing needed to be done and the fuss would soon blow over. Unfortunately, there was a technical fault with the recording system so that that episode of conversations was never recorded; and in legal speak therefore never took place.

Over the next few days Nixon also reluctantly agreed to pay money to the arrested conspirators in order that their families would be taken care of and not suffer unduly from their arrests. Nixon, ultimately, was a kind man and loyalty to his team had been his hallmark in public life. That was his second big mistake. The discussion had been recorded by his taping system which had been repaired. That tape was to constitute one of the pieces of incriminating evidence for a cover-up. Unbeknown to the Nixon team they had walked into a trap with no hope of escape. It was the beginning of a two-year plot of a slow drip-drip of incriminating evidence. Of course, the payments to the raiders' families would be interpreted as payments to buy silence and therefore evidence of a cover-up.

.

CHAPTER 9 - SARAH CORNFIELD

Sarah was attractive but was not what one would describe as a ravishing beauty; she had a certain charm or charisma and was regarded by her peers as having an attractive and bubbly personality. She was a very open and likeable person and had very wide and varied circles of friends. In fact she could be said to have many circles of friends and acquaintances. Sarah had friends to exercise with; others to discuss her interests in political journalism, progressive books, and music. She was able to keep each circle of friends separate. Sarah had pale green eyes that sparkled, indicating the immense life-energy in her. She had a dainty mouth like a rosebud and a slightly pointed nose, but not a ski-slope. She had long blonde hair tied up in a pony tail that was so fashionable in the sixties and early seventies. The big hair-do of Farrah Fawcett of the mid-seventies had not yet been fashionable. She would wear heels, especially to more formal functions, but preferred to wear the less attractive flats and unfeminine trainers. She listened to Bob Dylan's 'Blowing in the Wind'; Joan Baez's 'We shall overcome'; Peter, Paul and Mary, but did not know what was being alluded to in 'Puff the Magic Dragon'[1], being rather naïve on the drugs front. She had never touched pot or LSD or such mind-altering substances. She also listened to Simon and Garfunkel and was enraptured by the film *The Graduate* starring the young Dustin Hoffman and Anne Bancroft. Although her taste in jazz and classical music was limited, she knew of the work of Dave Brubeck, Thelonius Monk and Mile Davis, Mahler, and Shostakovich and even Berg. Her taste was pretty eclectic as with most of the young in the sixties.

Although she did not think so, Sarah was politically rather naive. Posters of Senator McGovern, the Democratic presidential peace candidate against Nixon hung alongside that of Ché Guevara on the walls of her bedroom cum study. She had read Eldridge Cleaver, Stokely Carmichael and James Baldwin's *The Fire Next Time*. She had cried when Martin Luther King Jr. was shot in April 1968, although she did not really know why. She had also read Simone Beauvoir and Jean Paul Sartre. She sympathized with the blacks intellectually but did not socialize with them. Her involvement with the black movement was thus quite superficial.

She had also read Regis Debray and Franz Fanon[2], intellectual leaders of the fight for freedom in Latin America and Algeria at the time and whose writings were published widely in the US and Europe. They were deemed to be less of a threat than the classical communist literature. It had become fashionable to be seen around the campus with a copy of *Wretched of the Earth* by Franz Fanon or books by other left wing writers. It mattered not whether the students were politically aware and active. One had to be seen to be in tune with the times. As even the arch-conservative Winston Churchill was alleged to have said, 'If you are not a liberal at twenty you have no heart, if you are not a conservative at forty you have no brain'.

Sarah had been to sit-ins; discussed Marcuse[3], especially his books the *One Dimensional Man* and *Eros and Civilization*. She generally felt good that she had a progressive outlook, but did not really know what it meant in practice. She was radicalized when her brother ran away to Canada to avoid the draft to fight in Vietnam. The Vietnam War was the trigger to her limited radicalization. Her experience was therefore much like that of many other young people of that era.

Sarah's father, Jack Cornfield, used to work in the Marine Corps Intelligence Service. Her parents were conventional Americans of the era, bewildered and estranged from the young more through their inability to understand what the young people were about than from anything else. They had moved to California although they had spent their youth in the East Coast. Washington DC was in fact where Jack Cornfield had been a major with the Marines Intelligence Service. They had moved to California to be with their daughter Sarah when she won a place at Berkeley to major in journalism. The move was no big deal as Jack Cornfield had recently retired but had retained his network of friends and colleagues in the Service in the East and West Coasts and other parts of the country. It was a bit more difficult for Madeline, his wife. She had felt wrenched from her friends. Being a person with an optimistic disposition, she soon got over it and now five years later had a wide circle of friends and had even developed a reputation as somewhat of a social butterfly.

The Cornfields were a patriotic family, which was not surprising as Jack had served in the Marine Corps Intelligence Service and had risen to the rank of a major. They believed firmly in the American ideal of 'motherhood and apple pie'. It was therefore quite a shock when Jimmy, the elder boy refused to report for the draft and ran away to Canada. That was some four years ago. They still kept in touch, although very sporadically. That event was very traumatic. Jack, although he would like to see Jimmy join up, was also fearful for his well-being. There had been so many reports of young American boys suffering severe injuries. The number of body bags of young Americans had increased. According to the latest reports, some 40,000 young American servicemen and women had been killed. The number of service personnel maimed would run into hundreds of thousands. The issue of the draft had almost torn his family apart. Madeline was quite clear that Jimmy should not join up and put his life at risk. 'Why are our boys being sent thousands of miles away to fight a war that I just do not see the point of? It is not as if Vietnam is Mexico just south of our border or even Cuba.' Jack's position was very ambivalent. He could understand and empathize with his wife over her concern but his sense of duty to his country told him otherwise.

The dilemma in fact was 'resolved' when Jimmy took off to Canada. Jack loved Jimmy dearly, and through his contacts had even arranged a way to periodically send money surreptitiously to him. He knew that he was working as a farmhand in the Canadian prairies. Although he could not be sure, he knew that Jimmy was safe.

The incident had changed Jack's outlook. He had been a non-committed Democrat and had given them his vote all his life. Jimmy 'dodging' the draft had drastically changed his political views. The most urgent issue facing the country was Vietnam, and he would vote for anyone who promised to pull out of Vietnam. He had become a staunch supporter of the Nixon doctrine to let 'Asians fight against Asians'. The Vietnam conflict had nothing to do with America if one did not believe in the domino theory that was propagated by the Democrats and Kennedy in the 1960s. The Americans had been in there for more than eight years with nothing to show for the blood and treasures expended. Thus he had voted for Nixon at the last election and would vote for him again. Although from his service days he understood that such things move slowly at their own pace, he had recently felt rather disappointed that young Americans were still dying or being wounded in Vietnam. However, he supported the concept of Peace with Honour as the only way to extricate America from Vietnam. Given the circumstances, the Cornfield seniors would not hesitate to stand by their kids as parents do. They thus had unstated sympathy with the students after the shooting and killing at Kent State University, Ohio on May 4, 1970.

Sarah was never a member of the Students for Democratic Society (SDS)[4] but through her days at Berkeley was familiar with their views, which were anti-racism, anti-draft, and anti-war, in particular the Vietnam War. She sympathized with the faction of SDS that was anti-communist. Sarah did not like to be labeled as 'part of the problem'. She had aligned herself to be 'part of the solution'. Thus, she had participated in the anti-Vietnam War demonstrations, especially during the recent incursion into Cambodia. She was aghast by the shooting of the innocent students at Kent State University by the Ohio National Guard on May 4, 1970. She had participated in the national demonstrations against the shooting after that. The motivation was very much to do with self. She could see that it was now possible to be shot and killed by American soldiers while in mainland America. It was no longer safe to be a citizen of the United States of America. The demonstrations were expressions not only of anger but also of a very deep-seated sadness of what was happening to her beloved country and fear of personal injury. Thus her politics were very much that of a female petty bourgeois intellectual. She had been brought up to think for herself and was a natural skeptic but was imbued with a deep love for her country. She was a troubled young woman.

Although she was not particularly academic, Sarah had quite a good head for books and majored in journalism at Berkeley University from where she got her left-leaning outlook. She graduated in 1969, did two years internship before landing the position as a rookie investigative journalist at *The Los Angeles Times*. She was not particularly confident at the job interview but managed to charm the executive editor into giving her the position. Being friendly with Paul Conrad, the famed Pulitzer Prize winning political cartoonist must have helped.

CHAPTER 10 - THE ASSIGNMENT

It was the winter of 1972/73 and Sarah Cornfield had been on the job with *The Los Angeles Times* for some nine months. She was not doing anything particularly exciting. She had had only one major assignment but did not even get a byline. Sarah felt that her career was at a *cul-de-sac*. She was not prepared to accept the situation and had decided that she must grasp her destiny with both hands and had come up with a very audacious idea. Sarah, like many of the millions of young American youths, had been fascinated by the detailed reports by Carl Bernstein and Bob Woodward emanating from *The Washington Post*[1]. She had made an appointment to see the editor of her newspaper with a very bold proposal

She knocked and, when summoned, walked into his office, the hallowed chamber where editorial policy was determined. There was the smell of leather from his desk, chairs and loungers mixed with the aroma of cigar smoke. It was warm and cosy. She was invited to sit down. Although she had written everything down in her folder, she decided to speak on her proposal rather than to read it, as she thought it would make a better impression.

She started, 'Sir, I should like to propose that I go to Washington DC on a non-attributable assignment to investigate what is behind this Watergate affair. It has been running for quite a time and the amount of details in those reports read like the 302 FBI interrogation notes. I have a feeling that there is more to the official story than meets the eye. I have a hunch that there is a big story behind all the tittle-tattle.'

His curiosity whetted, the editor said, 'I see, tell me about your proposal.'

'Well,' she said, 'I should like to go to Washington DC for at least six months to see if I cannot break into *The Washington Post* circle and come up with a different story. It will be a non-attributable assignment and I shall be there completely anonymous, with no linkage to *The Los Angeles Times*.'

Sarah continued enthusiastically, 'I have summarized the reports from the Watergate break in which was first reported on June 17, 1972.

'Why did a burglary at the offices of the Democratic National Committee at Watergate take place when Nixon was ahead at the polls by at least 26 per cent? What were the four Cubans among the arrested doing? How come they were caught? From all my reading, the break in was a fairly routine job of surveillance, but it was the third attempt to break into the Democratic National Headquarters at Watergate. Then there were all the incriminating $100 bills with consecutive serial numbers, very strange and incriminating and therefore unrealistic. Next was the story that Howard Hunt ex-CIA, had his name and contact details in the address books of two of the charged Cubans. It was as if evidence had been planted to lead the investigations along a certain direction.

'There was this slush fund that was overseen by John Mitchell, the Attorney-General and Maurice Stans, Nixon's assistant. There was supposed to be in excess of $300,000 in Maurice Stan's safe and $25,000 in dollar bills had been given to the Cubans and an unspecified amount to Howard Hunt. I would have thought that all campaigns have slush funds. On October 24, 1972 *The Washington Post* had openly accused Bob Haldeman, the White House Chief of Staff, of doling money to the Watergate convicts to buy their silence. By the end of October, there were many more Watergate-related stories up until Nixon won his re-election by some 60 per cent of the popular vote. This was followed by a report in January 1973 that John Dean, the White House Special Counsel, was reported as saying, shortly before Nixon was to make his inaugural speech for his second term of office, that Charles Colson, a White House aide, was having problems with Howard Hunt, one of the men arrested at Watergate.

'By February 1973, the Senate had voted to form a committee to investigate the Watergate affair. This was soon followed by the testimony of Patrick Gray, the acting director of FBI, in which he was reported to have testified that John Dean, the White House Special Counsel, had access to the Watergate reports.

'Why would the Nixon administration bring in the new Campaign Funding (FEC) Act to increase accountability and transparency if they were working against the law? It just does not make sense to me. However, the conventional story suggesting the abuse of presidential power and cover-up has been published and like other memes have developed legs of its own.

'The reporters of *The Washington Post* had used the specific case of the Watergate break in to generalize the issue to bugging, surveillance and dirty tricks in general and then went on to develop the story into another specific area of the Nixon campaign. It is this second specific area that I am not completely sold on. There are other possibilities that have not been investigated. What if the break in was a setup? Both sides can be involved in dirty tricks. As you know, I am no supporter of Nixon and given the chance would vote him out. But looking at the situation objectively, I do not think that the story being unraveled by *The Washington Post* is necessarily the only one in town. I would like to have your permission to go to Washington to see if I cannot piece together another story. It just does not make sense to me. Nixon's campaign was miles ahead according to all the polls. His campaign had nothing to gain from such a foolish scheme and Nixon is not exactly a fool.'

The executive editor paused for a moment in deep thought. There was the possibility of an alternative version of the story and young Sarah might have put her finger on to it. If the possibility turned out to be true, *The Los Angeles Times* would have a blockbuster scoop, maybe even a Pulitzer Prize. He raised his head and looked straight into Sarah's eyes, 'You mean non-attributable? You would be completely on your own in this investigation. It may be a dangerous assignment, because if there is any truth in your hypothesis, then very powerful people are involved. I am sure that you are plucky enough to do this, but in view of the dangers, are you sure you want to do this? If you were my daughter, I would want to talk you out of this assignment. However, I am also wearing the hat of the executive editor of *The Los Angeles Times* and I cannot pass over the possibility of a major scoop for the paper. OK, I will sanction this non-attributable assignment with reluctance.

'You will have to take on another persona. You will be paid by a secret account in cash, left for you in a safe drop box that we use. Our security people will brief you on the details. When do you plan to leave?'

'I plan to leave as soon as possible. I will get an apartment. Please don't worry, I shall be very careful and I will be all right. Don't forget that I grew up and lived in the East Coast before coming out to Berkeley and then joining your outfit.'

CHAPTER 11 - SARAH IN WASHINGTON

Sarah, very excitedly, dropped a hurried note to her mother saying that she would be out of Los Angeles for a few weeks. It had something to do with work, but she did not expand. She now had the chance to get the scoop of her life, an assignment that could change her career path completely. She paid for her Pan American air ticket in cash. She did not pay by cheque, as that might be traceable, and used the pseudonym S. Cunningham. The flight would take some six hours. She planned to stay at the Holiday Inn hotel initially until she found an apartment.

Sarah had chosen the Holiday Inn on Rhode Island Avenue near the White House, between 14th and 16th Street NW and therefore near the offices of *The Washington Post* which was on 15th Street NW. Her choice of hotel was not the cheapest. She probably could afford a week's room hire. It was not extravagant. Sarah felt that she needed to orientate herself as it was some years since she had visited Washington DC. She was a schoolgirl then and had been out on a trip to visit the capital city. After a fleeting tour when they saw the White House, the Washington Monument, the Capitol and the Lincoln Memorial she had spent most of the day at the Smithsonian Museum as it was a science class outing.

The next few days saw Sarah exploring Washington DC like the college girl she had recently been. She made it a point to be familiar with the likely places that Bob Woodward and

Carl Bernstein would hang out. *The Washington Post* offices on 15th Street NW were very sparsely served by bars. The little bar across the road some two hundred yards down the left was the only place that tired reporters after a day's work could hang out for a drink and chill out before heading off home.

During the day, she looked at the classified ads for inexpensive apartments on term lets. All the central apartments were rather expensive. The ones she could easily afford tended to be far out in Virginia where she once lived. She soon realized that if she took a cheaper apartment out of town she would have to consider the time wasted on travelling and the cost of cab fares. She therefore decided to compromise and settled for a tiny apartment across the river in Columbia Plaza near the George Washington University campus and only some six minutes from the Watergate complex. It was near to the centre of Washington DC. She put down a deposit for six months. She had reckoned that she would either come up with a lead or draw a blank by that time. She had not got in touch with any of her friends as she did not want it to be widely known that she had returned to the East Coast, as it might break her cover.

In the evenings, she took on the persona of a different person – an attractive young woman, new in town, looking for some action. She let her hair down, put on lipstick and wore the short dress that she had bought from Macy's when she was last in New York. It was a short, scarlet, body-hugging number and therefore rather sexually provocative. It had been her twentieth birthday present to herself when she had decided to splash out. The dress was probably the most feminine outfit she ever had. Sarah was careful to make sure she did not look like a tart. While it might not put off Carl, she was not sure of Bob Woodward's taste in women. She had to make sure that she was in a position to lure either of them to her honey trap.

For about a week she went to the little bar opposite the offices of *The Washington Post* and waited from about 4.00 pm till past the rush hour. On certain evenings she would be at *the* bar from about 9.00 pm and stay for an hour in the hope of 'accidentally' bumping into one of the Watergate reporters. She knew that it was the watering hole for *The Washington Post* journalists from the chatter around her.

Sarah was reading everything she could lay hands on about the Watergate affair. She studied the daily copies of *The Washington Post* and *The New York Times* and other papers at the local library. She made detailed notes and digested everything she had read. Thus she had on record the date and source of every item ever published on the Watergate affair. She had so immersed herself in the accounts that she had become a walking encyclopaedia on Watergate. There was no report that she could not quote back almost verbatim. All these notes Sarah kept in a little book that she always had with her.

That evening, Sarah was quite dejected. She had been in Washington for several months. Summer was already ending and fall was fast approaching, with the characteristic chill in the air especially in the evenings. Although she had been working very hard, she had not been able to get any useful leads although there had been several more Watergate-related reports in *The Washington Post*. She had even tried to use her feminine charms on Carl Bernstein with no success.

They had a 'chance' meeting one evening several weeks ago in the bar opposite the offices of *The Washington Post* on 15th Street NW. She had been hanging out there for several nights already, hoping to engineer a chance meeting with either Carl Bernstein or Bob Woodward. When she did her research, she had felt that she might have a better chance with Carl who had a reputation as a ladies' man. Sarah had untied her long blonde hair that flowed over her shoulders. She was wearing lipstick and heels rather than her usual sexless trainers and had sat at the bar counter in a slightly provocative manner. From the corner of her eyes she noticed that a few of the men present had given her several come-hither glances. She was sure that one of the men would make a move on her, when in bounced Carl Bernstein. She recognized him instantly from the photographs she had seen of him. He seemed rather full of himself, waved at the crowd in the room and made his way to the bar counter where he ordered a shot of Jack Daniels. He had noticed Sarah and inched his way towards her.

He greeted her with, 'Hi, new here?'

'Yeah, I got in a couple of weeks ago.'

'Erh!'

'I am a journalist student looking for an internship. You must be Mr Bernstein, aren't you? Your stuff on Watergate is quite awesome. Can you help me?' Sarah had decided to grasp the bull by the horns and go for the kill immediately.

'Chucks, it's nothing. Just routine, digging around; pays the bills.' Carl ignored the request for help but was happy to receive the compliment about his Watergate reporting, at the same time playing down its importance.

Sarah shifted on the bar stool and in the process pulled her skirt up a bit more to reveal even more of her dazzling white and luscious thighs, between her suspenders and her stockings. She could sense that Carl was interested and was being only mildly encouraging. She must not be too obvious with her honey trap in case he smelt a rat.

Carl approached her slowly and drawled, 'How about I got you a drink?'

She accepted his offer demurely and waited for his hit. Unfortunately, rather out of character, he did not make a move on her. He soon left the bar, to her disappointment.

CHAPTER 12 - LUCKY BREAK

Feeling rather depressed, a few weeks later, Sarah made her way to a café-bar at the outskirts of DC a few blocks from her apartment. She ordered a Bud more to drown her sorrow than to quench any thirst. She had to review the activities of the past few weeks. The inside of the café-bar was warm and filled with cigarette smoke. But it was not the best place to conduct a self-evaluation. It was cosy – a juke box in the far corner by the bar was playing Simon and Garfunkel's hit song 'Bridge over Troubled Waters'[1] which ironically was quite apt. She had to decide soon whether to call off the assignment and return to Los Angeles. She had been there for some ten minutes when in walked two men. She immediately recognized one of them as Bob Woodward, *The Washington Post* journalist who, together with Carl Bernstein, was causing quite a stir with their Watergate reports. From the reports carrying their byline, they had such detailed knowledge that they must have a very good source. *The Washington Post* in September 1972 had referred to their source as 'Deep Throat'[2].

She tried not to look at them as they went up to the bar counter, ordered a drink each, sat on the bar stools at the far end and went into a huddle. The November 1972 presidential election was over and Nixon had won a resounding victory. The US electorate must approve of what he had done during his first term. Nixon had clearly thrashed the wishy-washy Senator McGovern, the Democrat candidate for the presidency. Nixon had won by 60.7 per cent – the largest popular vote in US polling history: a record. Maybe his guard was down in the euphoria following the presidential elections.

The two men chatted for some twenty minutes with Bob Woodward occasionally glancing around furtively. He was obviously uncomfortable and uneasy to be seen in the open with his companion. Sarah decided that night might be her lucky break. She had to follow the other man as he could be a lead. She was done following Bob, something she had carried out on many occasions since her arrival, with nothing to show for her efforts.

She slowly got up, left the café-bar and waited outside in the dark shadows across the street, far enough not to be seen, yet near enough to recognize the people as they came out of the café-bar. Having waited for more than fifteen minutes, she noticed that one of the two men leaving the café-bar was Bob Woodward. The men parted company, and after a reasonable interval, she walked out to follow the other man. Sarah was beginning to feel nervous. What if it was a trap, or what if the man was already being followed by Nixon's cronies? She might get in the way and be an innocent victim.

She pulled herself together and told herself not to be so silly. Nixon had won the election by a massive margin and was unlikely to pay much attention to the Watergate story which after all was only one of many incidents during the election campaign.

Nixon's campaign headquarters in Hollywood and in Phoenix had been subjected to arson attacks during the election campaign. It looked as if both sides had been playing dirty tricks against each other. There had been no arrests and no fuss made and yet so many column inches had been devoted to Watergate. Something was not right. She just could not believe that the Democratic Party did not indulge in dirty tricks. The Kennedy family was notorious among those in the know for being ruthless exponents of dirty tricks.

She kept her distance from the mystery man, who seemed to know what he was doing in taking some evasive actions in case he was being followed. Sarah's pulse raced. He must be an important lead if he could demonstrate professional proficiency in evading surveillance. She must have followed him for more than six blocks when he suddenly turned into a town house, ran up the steps two at a time, opened the front door and disappeared. The lights on the first floor came on and he did not emerge even after ten minutes. She gave herself another ten minutes before emerging from the shadows to get the house number. By that time she had decided to seek the help of her father. With his impressive expertise from his days with the Marine Intelligence Service, he was the very person to help her trace the stranger. She would do that first thing the next morning.

She slowly started her journey home, feeling excited and also somewhat elated. She felt in her bones that at last she had found a lead. All she needed to know now was the identity of the person and then work her way from there.

She decided to be extravagant, hailed a yellow cab to take her to her little apartment.

The next morning, she had a lie-in before phoning her father. 'Hi Daddy, I need a big favour.'

'Sure honey, how are you? Where are you calling from? What is it you want?'

'Daddy, I am sorry I cannot talk now. I need you to find out the identity of the person living in this address,' as she gave her father the house number and the name of the street. 'It's for one of my *Los Angeles Times* research assignments. You can call me on my phone,' as she gave her father the telephone number of her small apartment.

Later that afternoon, her reading of the day's *Washington Post* was interrupted by her telephone ringing. The ringing tone sounded really loud, so much so that it made her jump. The reason was that although her little apartment had a phone no one had ever phoned her. She was working incognito. She rushed to pick up the receiver and was reassured that the voice at the other end was the familiar warm voice of her father.

'Hi Honey, I have got news for you. But what are you playing at? I hope you are not doing anything dangerous. The person living at the address is Jacob Holmberg, a very senior officer of the FBI.'

'Thanks Dad, that is most useful.' Then she lied to her father, 'I am not doing anything out of the ordinary; some routine research for my boss in LA.'

'But that phone number, it is a DC number.'

'Yes, I am in DC for a week for the paper. Nothing special. How's Mum and the dog?' changing the subject. They exchanged a few pleasantries and then hung up.

Sarah was amazed but not surprised by the latest Watergate-related news report in *The Washington Post*. It carried the headline: 'Nixon on the Warpath against The Washington Post.' The main story was that the Nixon legal team had sued *The Washington Post* for US$1 million for defamation. The juicy bit of the story was that Patrick Gray, the current acting director of the FBI since May 1972 when Edgar Hoover had died in his sleep, had been nominated by Nixon to be the next director of the FBI, passing over Mark Felt, the deputy director who had some thirty years' experience with the agency. According to the report, Gray had gone to the White House to ensure his nomination. The unattributed report even alleged that he might have threatened Nixon with not keeping the lid on the Watergate affair.

The report ended by quoting Nixon, 'It is a question of the integrity of the US government and loyalty.' Seemingly unbiased, the story had already planted the seeds of the idea that there had been underhand activities and a cover-up.

Sarah thought to herself. If this Jacob Holmberg was the source of information for *The Washington Post* reporters and was a senior person with the FBI, then there might be something in her hunch that there was rather more to the Watergate story. Suppressing her welling excitement, she decided not to file any story for *The Los Angeles Times* yet. She had got to find out more and verify her hunches from at least two sources. She was taught that at journalism school. Although not a conspiracy theorist, she had great faith in her feminine instincts. Her training as an investigative journalist had kicked in just in time before she got too carried away. After all, what could she write that was a proper story and not just a bunch of conjectures? Her editor would have a fit if she were to file a story that had not been verified. It might be nothing at all, and just a coincidence that she ran across Bob Woodward at the café-bar. But what was he doing there, out of the way from his usual watering hole? She needed to formulate a plan to find out more.

Sarah then had a crisis of conscience. She returned to her hunch. If what she had postulated was true, then was the press being manipulated to dethrone President Nixon? Whatever one thought of Nixon, he had been re-elected by a landslide victory. The American people had spoken. Was this a plot, a coup to rid America of President Nixon? Who was this person so high up in the FBI? He had such detailed knowledge of the goings-on at the White House? Sure she did not like Nixon; in fact she absolutely loathed him. However, whatever her feelings about the man, he was now the legal representative and leader of the American people. Nixon had been returned by a majority of 60.7 per cent of the popular vote in November 1972 – a record in the voting history of America. While she did not like the President this was a matter of the Constitution. She had been brought up to swear loyalty every morning to the US Constitution at school. To Sarah, the Constitution was the crowning achievement of the founding fathers, and represented everything that was good about the nation. She could not and must not allow anyone to bring down the Presidency, violate the Constitution whatever the reasons. This was treason. It was her duty to defend the Presidency. She reluctantly had to agree with the President. Nixon was correct when he said that he was in a fight to defend the integrity of government.

She then made up her mind to warn the President of the possibility of a plot and inform him of what she knew already. If she could convince the President, he could put the entire power of the state into the investigation. When the plot was unravelled, she would get an amazing scoop for her paper. Thus it would be a win-win situation; for her career, the Presidency, and *The Los Angeles Times*. Sarah knew where her self-interest ultimately lay.

Sarah walked two blocks to the telephone booth. She did not want to call from her apartment as the call could be traced. She was not ready for that. She got the telephone directory out and ran her index finger down the column starting with W and then WH and soon found the number to the White House switchboard which was 202 - 456 -1414. She thought to herself that it was only in America that a relative nobody like her could call the White House. She therefore had another reason to uphold and defend the Constitution. The only option opened to her was to warn the President. After all to be forewarned was to be forearmed, which was half the battle.

Sarah dialed the number and waited for the ring tone. The switchboard lady asked in a very bright and cheery voice, 'DC 1414; this is the White House, what I can do for you?'

Sarah told the lady that she had something very important for Bob Haldeman the Chief of Staff.

Sarah decided to put all her cards on the table and cut through the public relations crap and blurted, 'Please, I need to speak to either the President or Bob Haldeman. I have very important information to do with Watergate.' As she was on a non-attributable assignment, she could not say that she worked for *The Los Angeles Times*.

Like magic the voice changed and said very quickly, 'Please wait while I put you through.'

After waiting for what seemed an eternity, a strong, confident and raspy voice came over the phone. She heard, 'Hullo, this is Bob speaking, what I can do for yer?'

'Hi I'm Sarah; I have very important information relating to the Watergate reports for the President. I think there may be a coup attempt on the President.'

After a pause that seemed to last forever the voice spoke, 'I need first to check you out.'

'OK what do you need to know?'

'What is your Social Security number?'

'It is SSN 123123123.'

'And your address?'

'I am afraid I cannot tell you that. I am on a non-attributable assignment for a national paper. Do you want to hear me out or not?' Sarah decided to be more assertive. The ploy worked.

'OK, I need to meet with you to check out your story. When can you come to the White House? What about 8.00 pm tonight at the White House west entrance?'

Sarah very excitedly looked at her watch. It showed 6:30 pm. If she hurried, she would have time to shower, freshen up and still make it in time to the White House.

'I shall be wearing a white and blue scarf and a khaki waterproof coat,' volunteered Sarah, rather needlessly, forgetting that it was not a clandestine meeting and she would have to identify herself to the guards at the west entrance. She was already half out of the booth to go back to her studio apartment. 'Yes, I can get to the White House by 8.00 pm.'

Sarah took great care with the way she dressed. The short slinky number would not be appropriate. She decided to wear her usual outfit but smartly. She put on a new blouse, a pair of slacks, and also a pair of black pumps rather than the usual trainers. She wore minimal make-up, viewed herself in the full-length mirror in the bathroom and was satisfied with what she saw. She looked the part of a young independent-minded woman. She carefully got out her white and blue scarf, and slipped on her khaki-coloured raincoat. It was 7:20 pm by the time she stepped out of her apartment. She had given herself thirty minutes for the journey. The rush hour was probably over, but she did not want to take any chance.

She was in luck. She saw a yellow cab with the 'For Hire' light flashing coming her way. Waving it down, she stepped off the kerb into the cab as it screeched to a halt.

'The White House west entrance please,' requested Sarah catching her breath. She had not expected to be summoned so promptly. The Watergate revelations must have the White House worried; otherwise she would not be summoned so quickly and without a full security check

CHAPTER 13 - SARAH MEETS NIXON

It was almost the end of the early evening rush hour. Sarah tapped her fingers impatiently as the cab manoeuvred its way through the DC traffic. It was nearly eight o'clock when she finally got off the cab and ran towards the West entrance.

She announced to the armed security guard who she was and whom she was meeting. She was glad when the guard said, without casting a second glance at her, that he knew that she was on her way. There was a female guard who gave her a quick body search and passed her as unarmed and allowed her into the White House compound.

Sarah was shown to the security enclosure. In less than a minute a tall man appeared, well groomed and sporting a crew cut. He went over to her and said gruffly, 'I am Bob Haldeman; I understand you have important info for the President. Out with it and it had better be good.'

She started to narrate her experience to date. Just as she was finishing, in walked President Nixon. Sarah was quite overwhelmed by his presence.

President Nixon, walking in to speak to Sarah was not such an unusual event. On the evening of May 18, 1970, Nixon had spontaneously gone to speak to the students demonstrating at the Lincoln Memorial in Washington DC after the Kent State University shootings, accompanied only by his butler. When he finally left, he had said to the students, 'I know you want to get the war over. Sure you came here to demonstrate and shout your slogans on the ellipse. That's all right. Just keep it peaceful. Have a good time in Washington, and don't go away bitter.'

Unlike so many of the press descriptions, the President seemed a kindly man; rather like a father figure. He was taller than Bob and exuded a commanding presence. One could tell that he was in charge and used to being in charge. He went up to Sarah and shook her hands. Sarah was flustered and did not know how to respond. Was she supposed to curtsey before the great man or what? The President, sensing her difficulties, quickly put her at ease.

'Don't worry, my dear about etiquette; just tell me what you know.' It was clear that the President was keen to know if she had anything new on the Watergate saga. Sarah breathlessly recited her concerns again. She told the President as it was, without any embellishments, but emphasized that it was all based on a hunch until the previous evening and that afternoon. Nixon and Bob both made a sucking sound under their breath when she mentioned Jacob Holmberg. At the end of her narrative, as she gained confidence, Sarah even volunteered that she had not liked the President. Nixon ordered Bob to pull up two chairs and invited Sarah to sit down while he sat on the second chair.

Nixon started by thanking Sarah for being so forthright. 'I fully understand your anger and also the anger of so many young Americans.'

He then began to tell her the reasons for his actions. 'You must be a patriotic young lady otherwise you would not have bothered to come to see me. Let me tell you some of the problems I face and then you can decide whether I have any other options.' Nixon wanted to disarm her.

'As a patriot do you want to see America defeated and humiliated by the black pyjama-wearing Vietnamese? What will happen to our standing in the world if we were to pull out of Vietnam unilaterally as some sections of the political elite are advocating? It is a very different perspective when you are sitting behind the desk at the Oval Office.

'I know we cannot win the war. We should not be there in the first place. I am afraid that although we have the military hardware and might, we are not always right to be in South East Asia. Do you want to see America withdraw at any cost? I love America too much to let that happen. I want Peace with Honour. That is the only condition that will see the US pull out of Vietnam; at least during my watch. I assume that you can keep secrets. We have been holding secret talks with the Vietnamese in Paris through the good offices of our French allies. However, the Vietnamese communists want to have everything. They want to defeat and humiliate us. This is why we are bombing Hanoi and Haiphong. I want to show them that they cannot beat the might of the USA. I want to bomb them back to the negotiating table. Peace with Honour is the only way that patriotic Americans will end this terrible scourge on our nation.

'Why do you think I went to China? Do you think I was paying homage to some old grandiose revolutionary? I am trying to bring about a change in the world balance of power that will ensure peace at least for the next generation. My heart bleeds when I see young Americans traumatized by their experience in Vietnam. Who should I declare my public support for – the 45,000 young men and women who have tried to avoid the draft or the thousands of Vietnam veterans who are prepared to lay down their lives for this country? I know that the young people in the country just do not understand the rationale for the war. Surprisingly, while I do agree with them, the reality is that we are in Vietnam and I as the President have to find a solution. I have come up with an overall strategy to ensure Peace with Honour. The Nixon Doctrine and Vietnamization are parts of that overall strategy. If you have a better solution I should love to hear it. And if you can convince me that it is a better solution, you can bet your last dollar I shall do my utmost to implement it. I have to be the President in order to supervise an orderly pull-out of Vietnam. But in order to be able to do so and ensure the supremacy of the United States, I have to do distasteful things. That, I am afraid, is part of the job. It is because I articulate the feelings of most Americans that I have been able to beat Senator McGovern so spectacularly.

'My opponents are unhappy about the secrecy surrounding the arrangements for the China trip. You should read Sunzi's *Art of War* – the Chinese classic on a three cornered fight for supremacy. By reaching out to China, we keep the Soviets guessing about our intentions. The Chinese feel threatened by their erstwhile Soviet allies. That is why they initiated the 'ping pong' stuff. One has to look for the hidden message. Foreign policy should not be a guessing game, but this is the real world and I am afraid that is how the game of realpolitik is played. I seized the once-in-a-lifetime opportunity for a rapprochement. Only I, with the media-generated myth as a virulent anti-communist, can pull off such an initiative. It surprised so many people. You are familiar with how the press has become muckrakers. I had to begin the initiative in secret in order to prevent it from being sabotaged. Many people were angered. By going to China, I have surprised our enemies, chiefly the Democrats. I have pulled the rug from under their feet. Although the implementation had to be done in secret, I have always tried to be open about my ideas. Read my speech made in 1967 at the Bohemian Grove and also my article in Foreign Affairs. I am not doing anything I have not hinted at before.

'There are so many problems affecting our country. It is impossible to solve all of them. That is just not practical politics. I am a politician versed in the art of the possible. I have to pick the main trend affecting our country, as by solving the principal issue, some of the secondary issues begin to be solved as well. I have indicated that my first priority is to end the Vietnam War. The war has generated the economic crisis affecting so many of our people. Sure, the Military Industrial Complex has been enriched by the war. That is a given. The rest of the nation has paid for the war in blood, tears and treasure. The drug culture is also a symptom of the war. The disillusioned youths are relying on consciousness-modifying substance to distant themselves from the brutality of the war. It is a way of forgetting and escaping. While I know that the drug culture and protests will not solve the problem, I can empathize with the young people. Don't forget that I too have children and grandchildren. Despite the so-called generation gap, I love our young people if only because they are the future for our country. I do not run away from problems. I am not like my predecessor who unleashed the war and then ran away because he could not face the consequences. I am not like that. I take my responsibilities seriously and I won't run away until the problem is resolved.

'Another reason for the rapprochement is the effect it has on Vietnam, my first priority. The Chinese do not have to say or do anything. The fact that the President of the US has been to China will engender doubts about China's commitment among the Vietnamese. See how it all fits? Can you see the sense of it? There are many in DC blinkered by their greed. I am a man of peace. I hate to see our young being estranged and traumatized both physically and mentally. The divide between the generations is tearing the nation apart. I worry over it. I think about the problem, looking for solutions all my waking hours. My negotiations with the Russians to limit nuclear armaments are making good progress. You must have heard of MAD the acronym for Mutually Assured Destruction. Between the Soviets and us, we can blow up the world many times over. I have no wish for this to happen during my watch. I want my children and grandchildren and their children after that to be safe from such a catastrophe. The SALT (Strategic Arms Limited Talks) treaty that I have negotiated with the Russians is anathema to the Military Industrial Complex, a powerful group first recognized by Ike, my previous boss, as a potential problem. However, at present they cannot oppose the peace that I am offering, because it is what the populace want. They know that they will stand to lose billions of dollars if both the Soviets and we were to disarm. If there is a legacy from the Nixon Presidency, it will be the world peace that I have helped to bring about.' Nixon rambled on as he tried to convince Sarah and himself that he was doing the right thing.

'I should like to run through with you my thoughts about the malaise affecting our young people. I am most concerned about the dropouts and the drug culture. The way I see it, it is the fundamental disconnect between the ideals taught to our young and the realities they have to face in the real world. It is almost a cliché to say that one has to adapt to the real world. It is my belief that one has to change the system if it no longer serves our purpose.

'The American young have been brought up on a diet of idealism. They are idealistic sometimes to the point of naiveté. They believe literally in the ideals of the 'land of the free' and the saying, 'as American as motherhood and apple pie.' They have been taught to believe in clean politics, absolute honesty and fairness. Their so-called role models are Senator McGovern and President Kennedy. They are ignorant or may be ignorant of the wiles and dirty tricks of the Kennedy family and the Democrats. They admire JFK as a clean-living and honest president in contrast to Richard Nixon whom they ridicule as Tricky Dickie. What they do not hear about is the ruthlessness by which the Kennedy family would go about to achieve their aims.

In Sunzi's *Art of War* is the maxim, 'know your enemy and know yourself, you will win every battle.' That was written in 600 BC. It is a given that for any political party to win the presidency of the United States of America, spying activities on the opposition have to be implemented in order to know their next move. Countermoves can be in place only if such foreknowledge is available. Thus, it matters not whether it is the Republicans or the Democrats, both parties have to indulge in spying activities to get the advantage over the other side.

'Bugging, false flag actions involving the media or on the ground are therefore run-of-the-mill activities. Both parties have access to slush funds, separate from the official funds. I introduced the FEC Act to reduce such activities. At present it is not possible or realistic to curtail completely such shenanigans.

'The schools and colleges teach our young about the ideals of our country – you know "the motherhood and apple pie stuff". We do not prepare the kids for the tough real world. The real world has been based on competition since time immemorial. Countries and neighbours compete against one another. Wars have always been fought. That is what capitalism is about. Our schools have been subverted. Kids are being taught that the name of the game is to participate when the real aim of the game is to win. It is OK to dream utopian dreams, but one has to plant one's feet firmly on the ground. We are in this world to win, whether it is presidential elections or a war in some far-off land. I don't like the idea of war. Maybe I have also been subverted. I have tried to reduce the dirt in our electoral process. That is why I passed the Federal Election Campaign Act to limit campaign contributions. I want to make the whole process more transparent and accountable. There are limits to the amount of change that is practicable. Maybe I have not gone far enough, but I made the judgement that the provisions in the act is as far as it is possible at present to solve some of the existing problems. Is it not better to make improvements by small increments than not to make them at all? Is it not ironic that I have been accused of breaking the law that have been put in place by my administration? Presidential politics is a high stake game. That is why there is so much chicanery in the process. I have participated in many elections, two for the vice-presidency with Ike, and three presidential and one governor elections. I have had dirt heaped on me, but those are the rules of the game and our country would be stronger if we play according to the rules to win. I know what it is like to lose. I have been a victim twice and I can tell you that it is not a nice feeling – an overwhelming feeling of rejection. Our founding fathers built in freedom of speech as a means to keep check on the executive arm of the government. However, has the pendulum swung a bit too far, now that I have to initiate policies by a process that involves secrecy and subterfuge? Is the fourth estate too powerful? A case can be made that it has become too powerful, and not in favour of the general populace. For example *The Washington Post* has run a campaign against me for over two years. Yet it is impossible to have a referee. Who is to referee the referee? Our electoral system is about the best system devised by men, despite all its imperfections. That is the real world. We have to understand that there is a gap between the ideal and the real. The trick to winning is to be able to bridge the gap. Every citizen has a say; it is the combined opinions of each and every citizen that make the difference. But now the game has so escalated that even the authority of all the citizens is not enough. The winner is accused of "dirty tricks" and attempts to manipulate the electorate. Of course all parties carry out all such tricks to try to win, but at the end of the day, especially at the second term elections, people are making a judgement on what I have done, and not just what I said I would do. Of course in order to achieve those aims I may have to resort to subterfuge, but those, I am afraid, are the rules. It is a tough game – definitely not for the faint-hearted. I have been through hell to get to where I am today. The struggle has toughened me. What drives me on? I could have made much more money working as an investment banker. I want to make a difference to the lives of the average American person.

'Is it so bad to try to get an advantage over your opponent? It is a game that has been played over the history of mankind. I must say that Sunzi had distilled the issues aeons ago in his *Art of War*. The Democrats do it to us and we similarly do it to them. The problem is that the media appear to be on their side. It is a no-holds-barred game. One has to pick a side and then do whatever is necessary to win. I do not think the young of today are prepared for this reality. You came to me telling me that you loathe me. Yet you did come. That is wonderful and it is the ability to see the good in society that keeps me going. I am not afraid of opposition. We have to argue out the issues. That is the strength of our democracy. Despite the present divisions, I am certain that we shall win through.'

Nixon continued with his long soliloquy, going over all the old arguments. It was as if he needed convincing as much as he wanted Sarah to be on his side.

'Do you know that it is a given that all our embassies are bugged? We bug those of foreign countries and they bug ours. I will be accused of negligence if I do not order that the embassies of other countries and the United Nations and so on are bugged. They are trying to make a mountain out of a mole hill with Watergate. Is it a crime to get the better of one's opponent? That is what electioneering is about. If only bugging does not take place. But that is the height of naïveté and utopian thinking.

'My dear lady, while I run the risk of sounding condescending, can you kindly, advise me how to implement the withdrawal from Vietnam, nuclear disarmament, and rapprochement with China when I am being opposed from all sides? It does not help that our fourth estate will jump at any chance to report any news story. That is how our country has been organized, and we have to work within its rules. Let us dwell on the often misattributed Voltaire quote on freedom of expression "I disapprove of what you say, but I will defend to the death your right to say it". Think about it, think about its implications. I have held that belief ever since I was a young man. Therefore while I disagree strongly with whatever is being reported about me by *The Washington Post*, I will defend their right to do so. This is the simple truth and also the explanation for the need for secrecy. We pride ourselves on the freedom of speech, which sometimes takes the form of lying about our adversaries. That unfortunately is the price. We have to indulge in diversionary tactics. Politics is like being a magician performing on the world stage. The audience expects the politician to periodically pull a rabbit out of a hat. How can I do that, if I practise only what you have been taught in high school? You must know that a magician uses smoke and mirrors to make his tricks convincing. I have to do the same to lead the country.' Nixon looked a man in pain as with difficulty he spelled out his personal philosophy and his view of the world.

'I sometimes have to say and do things that I do not believe in order to be able to bring about the changes that I truly believe in. Take the case of Lieutenant Calley of My Lai. Of course he was wrong to massacre the innocent Vietnamese. But as President of the United States, I cannot say that in public. Hey, this is definitely something that is off the record. My dear, you have charmed me into indiscretion. But I have been struck by your youthful idealism and yet you have a sense of reality to come and tell me about your suspicions about Watergate. It sounds crazy and it is probably crazy, but that is the real world we live in. You either join in to change it from within or you become a hippy and opt out. You have probably gathered that in my opinion the second option is nihilistic and therefore serves no purpose. War has a brutalizing effect. I can understand why Calley did what he did. It is the emergence of the suppressed anger of seeing his good friends killed or maimed. It was a primeval reaction. However, it would be political suicide to either support or oppose him openly. If the aim is to ensure that he remains free, I can do that. I shall issue a presidential pardon in a few weeks. I have the constitutional power to do that, but legally I am afraid I cannot overrule the verdict of the courtroom. Poor Calley therefore has to be in jail for a short while. At least he will not rot in prison for several years. Can you see how I have to lunge to the right in order to deal a blow to the left? A great deal of politics is just such play-acting. The aim to achieve some improvement for the people and the country is a lofty one while the methods to implement those changes are something else. The only true way to judge a politician is not just what he says but what he does, with the caveat that what he says has to be achievable. I would rather a politician tells me and gives me a telescope to view the moon than the empty but exciting promise to take me to the moon because the first can be achieved today while the second is just daydreams and utopian wishes.

'I agree wholeheartedly with you that we have to get out of Vietnam. It was a wrong war. I do not want to play party politics with you, but it was the likes of JFK and Lyndon Johnson who got us into the quagmire of Vietnam. Do you think I enjoy seeing young Americans coming home in body bags? The Vietnam War is what Ike had coined, the Military Industrial Complex gone mad. Over the past ten years, those sons of bitches had made their millions from the war. Do you think they will take kindly to someone withdrawing from Vietnam at any price? In that respect, while I do agree that the United States is quite unlikely to win over there and therefore has to withdraw, we cannot withdraw at any price, if only to honour the already more than 40,000 young people who have died. The only option for the United States of America to withdraw is my solution of 'Peace with Honour'. In order to placate the right wing, I will have to bribe them with whole lot of cash. That is the domestic price and how politics works. One cannot have something for nothing. It is always a case of quid pro quo. You are a patriotic young lady; would you want me to end the war any other way? Do you know that each time we drop a bomb, someone in the Military Industrial Complex is putting some $1,200 into his bank account? I do not like having to change nappies for the Democrats. But right now, the reality is that we are there and I have a problem to deal with. This is why I have to bomb them to the negotiating table. You must trust me to do whatever is required for our country. God bless America.

'Only I, with the reputation of a rabid anti-communist can lead our nation to implement the four goals of:

- Withdrawal from Vietnam with Honour;

- Nuclear disarmament with the Soviet Union;

- Rapprochement with China;

- Sort out the economic mess of the country.

'I see it as my destiny to carry out these tasks for our country. Why else do you think I went into politics? Of course I've made the odd buck or two. Any politician worth his salt should be able to make some money. It is the nature of the game. I have worked all my life to become the president of the United States of America in order to do some good for our country – God bless America. I have had to endure humiliations of losing elections and being labelled Tricky Dickie. Believe me it hurts, even though I have grown a very thick skin. Life is not like a rehearsal. Every day is like the opening night and you get at most one shot at solving a problem. It is likely that I have made mistakes. Do you know that if 40 per cent of what I do is good for the country, then I am a good president? The worst president is one who does nothing to solve problems crying out for solutions. Even if I make mistakes, at least we can, if we as a nation want to, learn from those mistakes.

'The United States cannot be the global policeman. While I believe that is the case, I cannot announce that to the country and the world. I would be instantly discredited. I am of course playing a very Machiavellian game here. As long as I am the President, there is a chance that I can achieve what is right for the country – God bless America.'

President Nixon's ramblings about his personal philosophy, fears and hopes for the country had taken nearly an hour and it was getting late. Sarah did not want to hear any more of this tortured man's ramblings. She rose from her chair as if to leave.

'Mr President, I must say that I was simply not aware that you have, as it were, a hidden agenda. Thank you for taking the time to explain your actions, when you need not have done so. Reluctantly, I must say that I have to agree with you. You are most persuasive. That is why I must go now. I promise that I shall pass on to your team whatever information that I may glean.' She had almost sworn loyalty to Nixon; such was the charm and persuasiveness of the man.

'Bob, please alert the switchboard to accept all calls from Sarah. She should use an innocuous code to announce herself. One such could be "Venus is calling". In the meantime I shall get my boys to find out what Mr Holmberg is up to.

'Let us hope that we can catch the liberal opposition with their pants down. If we do that, these people will become the laughing stock of the entire political world.' With that, the President walked out of the security enclosure, where they had spent the last hour or so.

Before Nixon left, Bob had whispered, 'Boss, should we not get Sarah's contact details?' In a reply with a look of disdain Nixon had said, 'Look, she came here of her own accord. She is a good girl and I do not wish to frighten her by being too intrusive. She will be back if she has any news.'

Haldeman asked Sarah if she had the cab fare home. She nodded and was shown the way out. Sarah walked away as discreetly as was possible. It was good that the nights were drawing in as, although it was only 9:30 in the evening, it was already rather dark. Sarah presented a fairly nondescript presence as she made her way into the night. She used the two-cab routine to get home to avoid being followed.

It had been a very long and eventful day. She had been wowed by President Nixon. He was not the monster as described by the press. He did not swear once during his long soliloquy. She had been bowled over by his charm. Although she would never vote for the Republicans, she needed to re-evaluate her values and beliefs. Was her adherence to the Democrats a tribal instinct? Had her parents' values anything to do with her own values? Were they in fact the same? Sarah had to cope with the problems of the new era and therefore her values might seem different superficially.

Unbeknown to Sarah, she had been spotted by a man in a dark coat and dark glasses, who also disappeared into the shadow as she walked by to hail a cab, taking care not to get on the first available one. He had noted down the cab number and company, both pieces of information he had whispered into his bulky radio-telephone.

CHAPTER 14 - HOTTING UP

'Damn!' Senator (Big Bill) Defoe struck his fist against his desk top, ' I have a suspicion that one of our cut-outs had been compromised. That woman had followed him home. We have to work on that basis and be extremely vigilant. This is a ruthless game and the only game in town worth playing. We need to work faster. We must not lose momentum.'

Nick, who had been given the task to get rid of Nixon from the political landscape, murmured his assent. 'We had not counted on a prying brat of a woman. I know I should have covered all the bases. A prying woman was the last thing on our collective radar. Now that we have identified her, we have to decide what to do with her. Our sleuth has reported seeing her entering the White House. Should she be eliminated before she causes any more problems for us? If so, how are we going to achieve that? I am afraid we have to make decisions on the last two items.'

The group of men huddled together. Their murmuring, although unintelligible, could be heard for a while. After some fifteen minutes, the men got up and filed out of the room led by Nick.

Nick was aware that his mentor, William (Big Bill) Defoe was not pleased with the recent development. It was good that his place man was generating a steady flow of leaks. He now had to escalate the flow. More information had to be given out. Nixon had been re-elected by a huge majority of some 60 per cent, if he remembered the press report correctly. He must hurry or otherwise the media will move the agenda to something else. He knew how fickle the media could be. He had to review the situation and to maintain the momentum. He had to instruct the source that more information had to be brought into the public domain.

Nixon had yet to be drawn into the final trap. It would be terrible if he were to get away, having got him so close to the trap.

CHAPTER 15 - DEEP THROAT

It was past 2:00 am and there was just another hour before the deadline for the next day's edition of the paper. Bob Woodward had used his two-cabs cut-out and then managed to run to the underground car park rendezvous with Deep Throat. There had been the usual message of a clock-face drawing on the crossword page of his newspaper. Was it not lucky that just as he and Carl were running out of material that he had been summoned? He must on no account miss this rendezvous. He slowed to a walk as he approached the darkened pillar. He could see the glow of a lit cigarette and knew that his source was still there.

'Hi,' he greeted the source, 'sorry I am late.'

'No problem, at least you are here. I noticed that you boys are running out of puff. I thought I should provide some help.

'The report on Haldeman in October was poorly done. You nearly let the fish off the hook with a single leap. Please do not repeat such amateurish efforts ever again.

'The most important thing that you must report is that there are hidden tapes of recordings of all the discussions that had taken place at the White House. The system is being maintained by a few selected FBI agents. Otherwise only Nixon, Haldeman, and Butterfield know of its existence. Even John Dean did not know until a couple of days ago.

'The killer information is in these tapes. The Congressional Watergate Committee must be told and a campaign be launched for the tapes and their contents to be made public. And don't forget Howard Hunt and the link of the White House with the Watergate Cubans. Also follow the money.

'I must also tell you that Nixon is preparing to unleash his gorillas. When that happens, things will get nasty and even dangerous. Good bye and good luck.'

Woodward, who had been scribbling down the very crucial pieces of information, broke out into cold sweat when the warning that he might personally be in danger dawned upon him. He had been secretive up till now in order that he and Carl were ahead of the pack. Now, his deep cover source was warning him of possible physical danger. He must consult his colleagues at *The Washington Post* to decide what to do. The discretionary part of him said that they should call off the campaign. However, he did not like to be threatened, even if not directly. His source could not be playing games. As he walked out of the garage, making sure that he was not being followed, he resolved to consult his partner Carl and their boss Ben Bradlee.

Although it was late he took a cab to Carl's apartment, taking care to do a switch. He went straight into the kitchen and turned on the faucet and the radio so that any eavesdropper would not be able to hear what he had to say.

To the confused Carl, he placed a finger over his lips and whispered, 'We are in physical danger over the Watergate story.' Very quickly he informed Carl of the gist of what he had learned from his deep cover that evening. 'I think we should consult Ben and do it now.'

Bob bundled Carl, who at last was fully awake from his deep sleep, into another cab. They took the ten-minute ride to Ben Bradlees's mansion on the north side of town.

They rang the doorbell and waited. They rang again. Some five minutes later the door opened and there was Ben in his dressing gown, 'What the hell are you guys on about? Do you know what goddam time it is?'

Bob, putting his index finger over his lips, hustled everyone into the shadow of the house, so as not to be conspicuous from the road. 'We are in danger, let us walk to the garden and talk,' he whispered as though the whole place was bugged.

Ben opened the French window that led to the vast garden. The three 'conspirators' made their way into the garden where Bob repeated the information he had just received from his deep cover source. 'In view of the fact that we may be in physical danger from Nixon's gorillas, we have to decide what to do next.'

Ben Bradlees's eye lit up in anger. The sleep had been driven from them. He paused to gather his thoughts and then launched a salvo against Nixon. 'The bastards have taken legal action against *The Washington Post* and are claiming $1 million damages. This has now become not only a hot political story; it has become a fight for the survival of the paper. It is my view that we will engage with Nixon in this fight to the death. I have a personal stake in the matter as well. Back in the 1950s, Nixon had one over me about the Alger Hiss case. He won that round. We have enough material to ensure that we win this time. Well, Nixon has a fight on his hands. OK boys, go back to sleep. I personally would advise our proprietor Katharine Graham that we should fight on. She is a feisty one. I have no doubt that she will want us to fight on. However, if any of you two want to back out, I would understand. You can put your decision in writing by 9:00 am tomorrow or I expect the full story in tomorrow's paper, if not in the morning edition, the afternoon late edition. We have the makings of a major scoop here, boys.'

The next day's *Post* carried a front page headline: 'Dean alleges Nixon knew of Cover-up Plans'. In this most damning of reports, the allegation was made that on April 15, 1973 John Dean had a conversation with Nixon. In that conversation, John Dean had come to the conclusion that President Nixon had known of the cover-up of the Watergate arrest as long ago as in 1972

CHAPTER 16 - MUSINGS ON THE FOURTH ESTATES

Sarah was aware of the danger she might be in. She had left the west entrance of the White House, taking great care that she was not followed. She was reassured that President Nixon did not pressure her to give her details. He had left it to her to get in touch when she had more information. She hailed the second taxi, carefully avoiding the first which might have been waiting for her to emerge from the White House.

A few days after her meeting with President Nixon, Sarah was very troubled. She needed space to think the issues through. In order to be inspired, she took a cab to the Lincoln Memorial. She got off at the Memorial and could not help looking at the wise and serene face of Abe Lincoln gazing into the distance. She felt very troubled; had she done the right thing to tell President Nixon of her suspicions? She was rather taken aback at the rapid response of Nixon's White House staff. The Nixon White House must be concerned. What were they afraid of? Was there a power more powerful than the President of the United States? What was the ultimate role of the media in this high stake political battle? The Constitution has enshrined the role and power of the fourth estate. Was it the role of the fourth estate to campaign to drive off a President who had received a huge mandate from the electorate? To solve her dilemma, Sarah tried to remember the concepts she had learned from her readings of Thomas Carlyle who had declared the supremacy of the fourth estate as long ago as 1840. She also remembered reading Oscar Wilde's comment 'We are dominated by journalism.'

In her college, she had also been taught to differentiate between the fourth estate to emphasize the independence of the press with the 'fourth branch of government', which suggested that the press was not independent of the state. She was aware that governments try to manipulate the media in their favour, while the press tries to carry out impartial, responsible, and accurate reporting of the facts. Was the press becoming too powerful? Were the press barons dictating terms to the government of the day? Was the fourth estate becoming too powerful if it can manipulate the courts and the public to instigate a coup? Sarah could not decide whether the balance between government and the state had been distorted, with the press now calling the shots. She could see the advantages of a free and vigilant press on behalf of the common people. But had *The Washington Post* overstepped the mark? Was its campaigning against Nixon in the interest of the American people? Was it merely seeking the truth? Had personal vendetta anything to do with the press campaign against Nixon? A newspaper was supposed to report the facts while the editorials gave the paper's opinions. Was the Watergate affair anymore shocking than other presidential scandals? After all, not much was said about the Gulf of Tonkin Incident when the USS Maddox was alleged to be fired upon by the Vietnamese. Was Nixon right to say that his Chinese and Soviet initiatives had to be shrouded in secrecy as premature reporting by the press would scupper any hope of success? Was the press so powerful that it could influence national policies? Not only that, was it on course to mount a campaign to impeach the President? Should a free press have that amount of power? Sarah was acutely aware that at no time did President Nixon rail against the power of the press. He seemed to have accepted it as a given and was willing to work within the realities of the power of the press by adopting secrecy in his methods. In playing this cat-and-mouse game, was he opposing the power of the press and trying to negate it? She decided that she could not find a solution to these weighty problems even under the inspiring gaze of Abraham Lincoln.

   As it was close to midnight, she decided to call it a day. She walked slowly towards Henry Bacon Drive to the north of the Memorial, in order to catch a cab to take her back to her apartment at Colombia Plaza. As it was late at night, it took her only ten minutes to get home. This was quite a difference from getting to the White House when the heavy traffic added another twenty minutes to the journey.

As she approached the door of her apartment, she noticed that the piece of hair that she had placed across the door had fallen off. Had her apartment been broken into?

Just as she opened the door, a dark shadow approached her from within. Sarah screamed and ran out of the apartment. She ran down the stairs out of the building. She regretted not paying the $50 extra to have a porter. She could see that a man was coming after her. She ran down the road towards the shopping area.

The next thing happened very quickly, there was the popping sound of a gun with a silencer going off. Sarah felt a searing pain to her left shoulder as she was hit. The force was so great that she fell over. She could vaguely see a man standing over her. He blew a whistle and a car approached. She felt herself being lifted and placed in the luggage compartment of the car. Sheer darkness descended upon her as the luggage door was closed over her. She could feel the movement of the car for several minutes before passing out. The next time she woke up she felt the car falling. Then there was a splash, and the luggage compartment became covered with water. Sarah surmised that the car had been driven off the road, probably into the Potomac River. She had to get out if she was not to drown and die. There was no use shouting for help as the car was already drifting down onto the river bed. She got all the strength she could muster and pushed with her legs against the roof of the luggage compartment. Nothing happened. It was locked very securely. Sarah could feel the cold water rising rapidly. She took a deep gulp of air, but drank a mouthful of cold river water instead. Soon she was completely submerged. Her lungs were about to explode as she could not hold her breath anymore. She opened her mouth and swallowed a large mouthful of water. Weakened by the loss of blood from the gunshot wound Sarah soon passed out. The end came quite quickly. It was welcome and strangely peaceful.

CHAPTER 17 - THE COUP *DE GRÂCE*

Two week passed, then three. Soon it was a month and there was still no sign of Sarah. No phone calls. No left message. The White House's last line of defence had depended on Sarah's allegations of a coup attempt. The newspapers were braying for Nixon's blood. The situation was getting desperate.

'Mr President, I do not think we have much choice in the matter. In order to save the Presidency and preserve your achievements, I am proposing that Ehrlichman, Kliendienst, Dean and I resign.' Haldeman was prepared to sacrifice himself to save the Presidency.

It was a meeting of Nixon with his top advisors held at the office of the East Office Buildings and not the Oval Office as had been incorrectly reported.

'When the storm blows over, the President could issue a pardon to all of us. It only means that we have to endure being imprisoned for a few months,' continued Bob Haldeman.

'But won't resignation be a sign that we are all guilty of the charges?' interjected Ehrlichman.

'Bob, you are forgetting that for those of us who are lawyers, resignation followed by indictment and imprisonment would inevitably lead to disbarment from the Bar. This means our livelihood would be on the line. Under such circumstances, I am sorry I am not prepared to be the presidential scapegoat.' John Dean interrupted and revealed the gap that was to divide the inner sanctum of the Nixon White House.

'Mr President, can you please confirm that you have the authority to issue a blanket pardon for your loyal aides?' asked Ehrlichman, seeking clarification.

'Dean, what is your opinion on this issue?' asked Nixon, directing his question to John Dean, on what he considered to be a technical problem.

'Mr President and gentlemen, I am afraid that a President at risk of being impeached would have absolutely no power to issue pardons,' pontificated John Dean, the White House Special Counsel.

'John, are you sure of that? As far as my understanding goes, the President has power of life and death over any citizen of the United States,' countered Nixon, feeling rather irritated by John Dean's pronouncements.

'I am sorry Mr President, what you say unfortunately does not apply to a President facing impeachment.' John Dean was not prepared to give an alternative ruling or be overruled by Presidential dictate.

'OK, let us say that Bob, John Ehrlichman and Kliendienst were to resign. How would that affect the administration?'

'I would suggest that our combined resignations might not be regarded as confession of guilt. I shall issue a statement denying guilt and indicating that the act is motivated by a need to protect the administration and its achievements to date.' Bob Haldeman came back.

'Dean, what is your position?' Nixon directed the question at John Dean and assumed that all the others would comply with Bob Haldeman's proposal.

'Mr President, with the greatest respect, I cannot allow my future and that of my young family to be compromised by something that I was not a party to.'

'John, I, as Chief of Staff, should remind you that if you do not resign, I will have to advise the President to sack you,' Bob Haldeman was not prepared to compromise on what he perceived was a question of loyalty and principle. He abhorred John Dean's behaviour, which had no place in his book.

Ehrlichman and the others had decided that it was better to resign en masse than to face the inevitable sacking by the President. They all resigned on April 30, 1973, hoping to deflect some of the heat from the Presidency. In truth, it was very difficult to say which was the worse course of action: resigning en masse or facing the sack by the President.

Haldeman had urged Nixon to fight on. He felt strongly that they had only tried to contain the Watergate events from causing political damage, which was justifiable action for any political party. The media had accused the Nixon White House as being involved in a cover-up and obstructing justice and abusing the power of the Presidency.

'Mr President, you must fight this unjust character assassination. I firmly believe that we have done nothing wrong. The Watergate debacle was just so much tittle-tattle. It was a crazy scheme. Taken on its merits, it did not amount to much. The Democrats had done worse to us, burning down our headquarters in Phoenix. As Chief of Staff, all I did was to try to contain the situation, something any Chief of Staff worth his salt would do. I implore you to fight against this politically motivated lynching of your Presidency.'

'Bob, I thank you sincerely for your fine sentiments. However, as the President I have sworn to defend the Constitution. Without any cast-iron evidence that we are the victims of a plot now that Sarah appears to have disappeared without trace, to make that allegation publicly would tear the already divided country apart. Freedom of speech is very important in our Constitution and is also essential to our democracy. Although I may disagree with what the misguided press is doing, I cannot destroy it. That would go directly against the Constitution. This is something I cannot do. I love my country too much to risk its integrity. I have to be selfless and make a sacrifice like we all have to do at some stage of our lives. The truth will out. I have devised a way to ensure that the truth will be told, but maybe not in our lifetime.'

John Dean was sacked as he had denied complicity. On April 15, 1973 he had urged the President to make incriminating remarks. By then he was aware of the existence of the White House recording system and was hoping that Nixon would say something incriminating that he could use for plea bargaining. He was trying to protect himself. It was the sort of behaviour that Nick, the deputy head of the China Lobby had predicted. Haldeman was willing to be a scapegoat because he believed in what Nixon was trying to do. But there was gaping division in the Nixon White House. Even Ehrlichman, who had been with Nixon since the late 1960s, did not forgive Nixon for not giving him a presidential pardon. He just could not understand why a pardon was not in Nixon's gift. Nixon could have prevailed upon Gerald Ford, who would be the thirty-eighth President, to issue the pardon.

In June 1973, John Dean was reported by *The Washington Post* of accusing Nixon of a cover-up. By the end of August, Judge John Serica had ruled that the White House tapes could and had to be surrendered. On September 15, 1973, John Dean testified to the Senate Watergate Committee that Nixon had taken part in the Watergate cover–up for at least eight months.

In November 1973, Woodward was informed by a White House source of an eighteen and a half minute gap in the Nixon tapes that had been subpoenaed by Judge John Serica and were now in the judge's possession. It was alleged that Nixon had deliberately erased an incriminating passage on the Watergate affair. Of course Nixon could not confess that he was trying to preserve the integrity of the US government by not exposing a discussion on the Establishment's cover-up of the assassination of John Kennedy.

Hoping against hope that Sarah would surface, the Nixon White House held a last ditched defence of the tapes. Nixon maintained that the tapes were his personal property and that only he had rights over them. He did not want to destroy them against the advice of many of his aides, as that would be considered as surrendering to unjust pressure.

The battle over the White House tapes led to the sacking of Archibald Cox, the Special Prosecutor and the resignation of Eliot Richardson the Attorney-General who had refused to implement the order to sack Archibald Cox. Eliot Richardson had replaced John Mitchell who had resigned to spend more time with his mentally disturbed wife. Nixon secretly admired Eliot Richardson for resigning. It was evidence that the safeguards put in place by the founding fathers were working. He was quietly cheered even if the outcome was bad for his political career. He had to maintain an outward show of optimism. It was necessary to maintain the morale of the White House staff.

In November, a new Special Prosecutor Leon Jaworski was appointed to replace Archibald Cox. The Grand Jury summoned the Nixon tapes as evidence of wrongdoing. John Dean, the President's Special Counsel before his dismissal, was in the process of plea bargaining for a lighter sentence.

The net was getting tighter. On March 1, 1974, Haldeman was indicted by the Grand Jury. Other senior persons in the Nixon team such as Ehrlichman, Colson, Mitchell, Strachan, and Mardian were also indicted. The whole force of the judiciary were harnessed against Nixon. The Washington District Judge John Serica, the Watergate Special Prosecutor Leon Jaworski and the Senate Grand Jury were all out to get Nixon. By July 1974, articles of impeachment were passed against Nixon by both Congress and the Senate.

There were further attempts to locate Sarah Cunningham. It was then realized that a major mistake had been made at the meeting with Sarah. Neither Bob Haldeman nor Nixon had obtained the contact details from Sarah at the end of the encounter. Nixon had consciously not asked Sarah for her details as he was to confess later to Bob Haldeman who paid an unscheduled call to the White House, urging Nixon to fight on.

'It was one of my biggest balls-ups, not seeking contact details from Sarah. I did not want to frighten her and turn her against me. I thought that as she had contacted the White House spontaneously, she would continue to stay in touch. Bob, I am really sorry for making this cock-up,' Nixon confessed to his erstwhile aide.

Extensive searches were mounted initially in the DC area. Nixon's efforts were handicapped in that he could not call upon the agents from the FBI or the CIA. He had to use his own 'plumbers'. With his impending impeachment, he was effectively a lame duck with little political traction. It was an impossible task. Sarah seemed to have disappeared completely without a trace. There were no police reports of a missing young woman that matched Sarah's appearance in both the local and the national press.

The only hint of a possibility was a small apartment in Columbia Plaza that had been let to a young girl with the initials SC. However, there was nothing in the apartment nor was there a forwarding address. The rent had been paid for in cash and the girl had not been seen for several weeks. Another month's rent had already been paid.

'Sarah has gone missing. She is to be presumed dead. I never suspected that there would be a plot against me. That was remiss of me. I had sworn on my family Bible twice to defend the Constitution of the United States. Freedom of speech is a very important and essential part of our Constitution. What the press has done might be considered unfair and misguided and I do not agree with its action. But that does not mean that I can destroy the press with groundless allegations of a plot. Today, the press seems to be over-powerful, but this is just the natural ebb and flow of power. Because of the checks and balances written into our Constitution, the perceived imbalance will right itself. I cannot risk doing something irrevocable to our Constitution,' reflected Nixon to himself.

'The country is already badly divided, and unsubstantiated allegations of a plot would tear the country apart. As I am not prepared to see that happen, I am truly trapped. There is no Gordian knot to cut. It is easy to be wise after the event. But I shall be exonerated by history. One day it will happen. I shall make sure of that.

'Hi Al, did you get anything in your check of the personnel of the national and local dailies?' directed Nixon at his new Chief of Staff.

'Mr President, I did not know that there were so many major papers. I drew a blank with *The Washington Post*, and *The New York Times*. The closest was *The Los Angeles Times*, but its executive editor denied any knowledge of what I was alluding to. So it was a blank as well. I am sorry I cannot help you,' intoned General Haig. He had already come to the conclusion that Nixon was a goner and he was not going to be dragged down in a hopeless fight.

'I have thought about the possibility that she might have been a plant to confuse us. This so-called "hilarious" farce is turning out to be quite a nightmare,' murmured Nixon to himself as he thought aloud.

'Now that she has not shown up, we have to act as if she has never existed. I hate to hand over a victory to my detractors, especially when they are so wrong and just cannot see what I am trying to do for America. I am sorry not to have asked for contact details. Do you think she would have given it to us?' mused Nixon as he was about to embark on one of his famous soliloquies.

'Let us try to work this out. Sarah could have been a plant to create confusion in a very complex problem facing the administration. Or she could have been genuine. In which case, why has she been silent all this time? She may have turned against us. Somehow my gut feeling tells me that it is unlikely. Why then has she not shown up? She cannot substantiate her story or she has been eliminated. We have tried our level best to track down a young lady fitting her description but without success. Reluctantly I have to conclude that she cannot substantiate her story and might have gone home. That being the case, we are now in really deep shit. I have tried everything in my power to stay above the fray, but without any success. My detractors have set a trap for me and I have sleepwalked into it this time. I have sailed very close to the wind, including sacking the Special Prosecutor Archibald Cox. I was not surprised that Eliot Richardson had resigned over the issue. In a way, it says something about the check and balance that had been put in place by our founding fathers to protect the Constitution. I believe that the need to protect the Constitution is what they had intended, even if it ends up putting me in disgrace. I must remember what I wrote in *Six Crises* as long ago as 1962. I said that '"Selflessness" is the greatest asset a person can have during a time of crises.

'I have fought this baseless accusation long and hard. In order to be true to myself and to serve the country, I must face the temporary humiliation of being the first ever President of the United States to resign to avoid impeachment. I have thought long and hard over Haldeman's plea to fight the impeachment. First of all, I do not think the country can withstand a long drawn out constitutional crisis. The country which is already deeply divided will be torn asunder. Secondly, it is my task to protect the freedom of the press and protect our Constitution which is the final guarantee that our country will remain free. Freedom of speech and of the press is an essential component of the democracy that I so firmly believe in. Our democracy may be imperfect, but it is still the best system ever devised by man. Lastly, to be honest I am tired of fighting. Maybe my entire adult career has been a preparation for this eventuality. The truth will out. I shall make sure of that when the dust has settled. I will be exonerated and my legacy as a great American President will live on. It may take sixty or more years for that to happen. I have made sure of that by having a signed affidavit describing my account of the incident in a sealed document to be kept in my presidential library that will be opened on the sixtieth anniversary of my resignation. My only regret for not fighting is that I cannot promise Bob, John and the rest of my team a presidential pardon. I do not think it would be fair to ask Gerald Ford, who will take over from me, to issue my entire crew with a presidential pardon. It will make nonsense of our legal system, another legacy of our founding fathers.' Nixon by now was rambling a bit. It was clear that he had been under a lot of stress. Yet he seemed almost serene. It must be that he had made up his mind on a course of action.

'Al, you must never divulge that the girl has ever visited us. In a way, the fact that she has proved to be untraceable means that this account has to be kept a secret. It would be political suicide for you to make such a declaration. It would sound so far-fetched that you will be branded as having lost your mind.'

It was only when the conclusion was made that Sarah had gone missing, presumably dead or had gone home, that the drastic scheme of resignation by Nixon with a pardon by Gerald Ford was believed to be the best course of action. A few months later in the autumn of 1974, there appeared in the missing persons' column of *The Los Angeles Times* a short message: 'Sarah, please do get in touch, we miss and love you dearly. Mum and Dad (Madeline and Jack Cornfield).' Jack Cornfield, despite his intelligence connections and a suspicion that Jacob Holmberg and the FBI was connected had also drawn a blank. He was unable to establish anything concrete. The secrets of the plot were safe.

Nixon had to do something quickly. If Sarah showed up, Nixon was hopeful that there would be a way out. If he could provide evidence of a plot to unseat him, there would be eggs all over the faces of the liberal press. Once again he would make monkeys out of them. It had been several months since Sarah's visit and there was no trace of her. Who and where was she? What had happened to her? Holmberg had cast-iron alibis and could not be incriminated as the mole that had been responsible for the leaks to *The Washington Post* journalists. The whole trail had gone cold. It was as if the visit of Sarah Cunningham had never taken place.

On certain days, Nixon even thought that the whole episode was a hallucination based on wishful thinking. However, Bob Haldeman did confirm that it had happened. Nixon personally scoured through the pages of all the Washington dailies. He even went through the local rags but could not find any report of the death of a young lady. There was absolutely no trace of her. There were no missing person notices in the local police stations. Sarah had disappeared without a trace.

Strangely, Nixon felt very calm although the external evidence of stress could be seen on his face. He had aged over the past few months. Yet he was serene as he had made his decision. Nixon decided that the country had to come before him. He thought of telling Kissinger, swearing him to secrecy for at least sixty years. On the night of August 8, he summoned Kissinger who was now the Secretary of State to tell him of his decision and his reasons. However he had doubts about Kissinger's ability to keep a secret, despite the successes with the secret negotiations with China and the Soviet Union. He changed his mind at the last minute. He had assessed correctly that telling Kissinger would only be an ego trip. He would not risk his sacrifice on an unnecessary ego trip. He had a secret document drafted, signed and sealed to be kept in his personal library in Yorbo Linda, California, to be opened only on or after August 9, 2034, the sixtieth anniversary of his resignation. He had worked out that by that time all the major players of Watergate would be dead and the truth can safely be told.

He bade Kissinger goodbye and asked that, although they were of different faiths, that they both prayed together. Thus, both men of two very different faiths kneeled and prayed together, united by their shared love of their country, the United States of America.

The next day, August 9, 1974, two years after his re-election by a landslide, Nixon announced on television to the nation that he would be resigning his office. He had lost the fight of his lifetime in order to preserve the integrity of his beloved country. The China Lobby had won.

EPILOGUE

While all attention had been concentrated on the phone calls to the White House by Carl Bernstein and Bob Woodward, Howard Hunt and other players in the Watergate saga, little attention had been paid to an entry in the external telephone log of the White House dated April 20, 1973 at 18:20 pm, of a direct line call by a Sarah C from a DC phone booth.

Could things have turned out differently? The answer is probably 'Yes.' It was therefore a mystery, why Nixon did not just sacrifice the Watergate conspirators.

Maybe he was too preoccupied with the lofty issues of Vietnam, China, the Soviet Union, and the domestic economic problems. His aides had misled him that Watergate would turn out to be a storm in a teacup. He had taken his eye off the ball. Or was he trying to hold together what he believed to be the best in America, especially freedom of speech, even at the cost of his political career? In Nixon's view, his career did not matter a jot when compared to the history of his beloved country. His life's journey was that of the American dream – from a poor boy to the President of the United States. He might have weaknesses and might have made mistakes but nobody could take away his achievements.

In 1994, at Nixon's funeral in Yorba Linda, California, President Clinton, in the presence of four past presidents, Gerald Ford, Jimmy Carter, Ronald Reagan, and George Bush, personally delivered the eulogy and the nation's gratitude to a great servant of the United States

Watergate - The Political Assassination

NIXON - A BRIEF BIOGRAPHY

Richard Milhous Nixon[1] was born on January 9, 1913 in the house his father had built in Yorba Linda, California. His parents were of modest means. Nixon never forgot his humble origins even when he became a member of the Republican Party.

He went to law school at Duke University from Whittier College in 1937, and practised law in La Habra until the Pearl Harbour attack by the Japanese in 1941, when he joined the navy.

He met his wife Pat Ryan who was one year his senior and was from a similar background. Although she was christened Thelma Catherine Ryan, she liked Pat, the name her Irish father liked to call her. They had met in 1938 at a local theatrical group when they were auditioning for a play. Pat graduated with a Bachelor of Science degree from the University of Southern California the same year as Nixon from Duke. On their first ever meeting, Nixon was besotted and asked for a date. When he was refused, he famously remarked, 'You shouldn't say that, because some day I am going to marry you.' It was an early demonstration of Nixon's strong will power, intense passion, and tenacity to succeed. They were married two years later in 1940.

Nixon was very devoted to his mother who was a Quaker and a pacifist. He joined the navy, courting displeasure from his mother. Nixon had already shown that his devotion to his country would override all other considerations even at that young age.

In the navy, although he did not see combat, he rose to the rank of a lieutenant commander. He participated in the VE day celebrations attended by General Eisenhower, who was then the Commander-in-Chief of Allied Forces and under whom he was to serve as Vice-President.

He was elected in 1946 as a Republican representative for California's twelfth Congressional district and four years later in 1950 to the US Senate. His progress in the United States legislature was stellar. He achieved notoriety as a member of the Committee to investigate Un-American Activities. Nixon exposed Algers Hiss[2] to be a closet communist. Hiss had risen to a very high position in the US government and was a leading supporter of the United Nations. Although Hiss had denied the allegation, he was found guilty at his second trial. Nixon successfully got Hiss jailed for perjury.

This was against the presumption of many liberal intellectuals and media luminaries, in particular Ben Bradlee of *The Washington Post*, who was among Hiss' many friends and had written extensively about his 'presumed innocence'. When Nixon unveiled the true nature of Hiss, who had many influential friends in both the media and the Establishment; he had whipped up a whirlwind. The media writers had to pen apologies or acknowledge their mistakes to the American people. This humiliation was something that they would never forgive Nixon, even though he was just doing his job.

All that took place before the paranoid days of the Senator Joe McCarthy[3] era of the 1950s. There were mistakes made on the side of the extreme right which Nixon decried, but in terms of defending the United States of America against infiltration by international communism, he was proven to be right in going after Hiss. Through Nixon's thorough and relentless investigations, a Nixon hallmark, Hiss was found guilty of perjury by the Grand Jury despite an inconclusive outcome at his first trial. Chambers, the ex-communist who had originally made allegations against Hiss, was thus exonerated. Although, Hiss was found guilty of perjury at his second trial, it had been assumed that he was guilty of being a communist mole. The subtle legal difference had been blurred. Nixon gained notoriety at the trial of Algers Hiss. He had drunk from a poisoned chalice, an act that was to plague him for the rest of his political career.

Nixon was selected to be the running mate of Dwight D Eisenhower[4] in the 1952 presidential elections due to his right wing credentials. He became one of the youngest Vice-Presidents in recent history. He also won a second term with Eisenhower in 1956. This was despite allegations by the liberal press of impropriety with campaign funds. Nixon was able to absolve himself after his famed 'Checkers' national TV broadcast.

Nixon's presidential campaign against Senator John F Kennedy in 1960 was unsuccessful, as was his campaign to be the Governor of California two years later against Governor Brown. However, when President Johnson resigned in 1968, Nixon won the presidential election against Hubert Humphrey. Nixon instinctively knew that the presidency would be his when Robert Kennedy, the Democratic front-runner, was shot and killed at a rally on June 6, 1968.

When Nixon finally triumphed, he was known as the 'comeback kid'. He gave his first inaugural address on January 20, 1969 swearing on his family Bible to defend the Constitution of the United States.

As the thirty-seventh President of the United States, he had campaigned on the following platforms:

Ending the Vietnam War, not by any means or on any terms but through Peace with Honour. It was contrary to the position of most of the political elite who only wanted to pull out of Vietnam quickly and by any means.

Creating a new world balance of power through rapprochement with China. Nixon wanted to work for world peace for his children, grandchildren, and all mankind. He also wanted to end the dangerous and massively expensive nuclear arms race against the Soviet Union.

On the home front he had to deal with the financial crisis, arising partly from the expenditures for the Vietnam War. To do that he implemented the New Federalism, introduced wage and price control and ended the gold standard. He also enacted the Clean Air Act and created the United States Environmental Protection Agency.

He introduced a new paradigm in funding elections through the Federal Election Campaign Act (FECA), in limiting the size of individual contributions to $5,000 and more stringent disclosures.

Although Nixon was anti-bussing, he successfully completed the desegregation of schools in the Deep South, a leftover from the Johnson administration.

The Vietnam War had been going on since 1964, when President Ngo Dinh Diem was assassinated in the midst of a military coup during JFK's term of office. The number of American troops present on the ground had increased astronomically from 20,000 advisors to more than 500,000 military personnel within three years. The Vietnam War was not understood by the US citizens. President Johnson had declined nomination for a second term in office. This was due to the stress brought on by the violent divisions in America and the mounting number of deaths among young US soldiers. Opposition to the war by the young was increasing, with serious disconnect between the generations, even in usually conservative families.

In 1968, Nixon had what is today described as Obama's dream team following in the footsteps of Abraham Lincoln's Team of Rivals[5]. In his first term, to everyone's surprise, John Connolly[6], a Democrat, was made Secretary of the Treasury. Nixon revived the National Security Council system which had gone into abeyance under President Johnson, who preferred to make decisions with a small number of trusted lieutenants.

Nixon appointed Henry Kissinger initially to be the advisor to the National Security Council and later to be Secretary of State which made Kissinger effectively the Foreign Affairs supremo. He had been the foreign policy advisor to Nelson Rockefeller.

Nelson Rockefeller was the other Republican candidate for the presidency, by virtue of his position as the director of the Special Studies Project of the Rockefeller Brothers Fund. Nelson Rockefeller was a potential Republican candidate for the presidency in 1960, 1964, and 1968 when he lost decisively to Nixon.

Nixon, despite his terrible reputation with the media that had painted him as an ogre, had tried hard to be inclusive. He conferred with President Johnson and also his Republican rival, Nelson Rockefeller, before making major policy decisions. It is difficult to gauge whether his inclusive policy was motivated by the desire for unity or to avoid his enemies 'pissing into the tent', so graphically described by President Reagan years later. His eventual decision sometimes did not coincide with their opinions, but he, at least, had the grace to solicit their opinions.

It is unclear whether Nixon had confided in ex-President Johnson and Senator Rockefeller about his plans for China and the Soviet Union. It is most likely that he did not, as he was very aware of the danger of an untimely leak which could jeopardize his initiative, which had to be kept under wraps.

The most immediate task facing President Nixon was the resolution of the Vietnam War. He initially escalated the conflict, overseeing incursions into neighbouring countries, such as Cambodia and Laos. Nixon promulgated the Nixon Doctrine of supplying arms to US allies who would have to do the fighting themselves. This was in order to save American lives and limbs. His doctrine led to development of the Vietnamization programme whereby large numbers of Vietnamese were recruited into the South Vietnam Army (ARVN) and supplied with American armaments.

Journalists who were anti-Nixon at that time described the Nixon doctrine as 'Let Asians fight Asians'. Similar approaches are today being implemented in the war against the Talebans in Afghanistan. American military personnel were thus gradually withdrawn and Nixon successfully negotiated a ceasefire with North Vietnam in 1973, effectively ending American involvement in the war.

His foreign policy initiatives were largely successful; his ground-breaking visit to the People's Republic of China in 1972 opened diplomatic relations between the two nations after a break of some twenty-five years. Nixon initiated détente and the Strategic Arms Limitation Talks, (SALT)[7]; the first ever summit meetings between the US and Soviet presidents.

However, his foreign policy was neither without criticisms nor shortcomings. The revelations that the Nixon administration ignored reports it received of the genocidal activities of the Pakistani army in East Pakistan during the

Indo-Pakistani War[8] of 1971, attracted widespread criticism and condemnation both by Congress and the international press.

Nixon probably was prepared to overlook the alleged genocide as Pakistan at the time was an important conduit to China. He could not afford to rock the Pakistani boat, his most useful contact with China. It was an example of how Nixon implemented his geopolitical visions. It was a ruthless practice of realpolitik – not to mar the bigger picture by an intervention to resolve a smaller and peripheral problem. Unfortunately for Nixon, those foreign policy compromises in the form of turning a blind eye could not be made public. He therefore had to suffer the opprobrium of the media and the public, for an action that seemed reasonable, given the true reasons. However, it was a tactic that he could not reveal in order to safeguard his new foreign policy direction.

He also implemented the concept of New Federalism, transferring power from the federal government to the states; new economic policies which called for wage and price control and the abolition of the gold standard[9]; sweeping environmental reforms, including the Clean Air Act and the the creation of the United States Environmental Protection Agency; the launch of the War on Cancer, and War on Drugs, and reforms empowering women, including Title IX.

In 1972 he was re-elected by a landslide with 60.7 per cent of the popular vote, beating Senator McGovern by eighteen million votes, winning all the southern states and forty-nine out of the fifty-one states. He continued many reforms in his second term, though the nation was afflicted with an energy crisis. The energy crisis was the direct result of the US support of the Israeli army that was nearly defeated in the Yom Kippur War[10] in 1973. Saudi Arabia, in retaliation for US intervention, drastically increased the price of oil in protest. This action brought about tremendous strains in the economies of the United States and the West. It was the first ever demonstration of the power of OPEC.

Nixon died in 1994, having had to endure several decades of notoriety when he was the first ever President of the United States who had to resign from the Presidency or face impeachment. At his funeral he was honoured by President Clinton and four ex-Presidents.

NOTES

These notes have been compiled to expand on some of the historical and contemporary events mentioned in the story that may be unfamiliar to the reader. All the notes have been verified by at least two sources.

Prologue

1. Gulf of Tonkin Incident or the USS Maddox Incident took place on August 4, 1964 in which four North Vietnamese patrol boats were supposed to have attacked the two destroyers USS Maddox and USS Turner Joy. It was used by President Lyndon Baines Johnson to obtain Congressional approval to escalate the war in Vietnam. It was the first year of Johnson's presidency and he wanted to contain the Soviet Union's expansionist policy of the Cold War by a show of strength. This policy of containment was the practical enactment of the domino theory. The domino theory presupposed that the loss of Vietnam would lead to further loss of South East Asian countries, such as Thailand and Malaysia, to the communist bloc of the Soviet Union and Red China. President Johnson on the night of August 4, 1964 made his speech calling upon Congress and the American people to approve his escalation of the war effort in Vietnam. This initiative, unknown to Congress at the time, had already been tabled for consideration months before by Secretary of Defense, Robert McNamara. The US Congress gave its approval on August 7, 1964. Within three years the number of American servicemen had increased from 20,000

military advisors to more than 500,000 military personnel in Vietnam.

In October, 2005 *The New York Times* reported that Robert J. Hanyok, a historian for the US National Security Agency (NSA), had concluded that NSA deliberately distorted the intelligence reports that it had passed on to policy-makers regarding the August 4, 1964 incident. The question can be raised whether President Johnson told a deliberate lie to Congress and the American people in order to obtain Congressional approval for the escalation of the Vietnam War, which is now termed by the Vietnamese as the US War in Vietnam. Over three million Vietnamese and more than 50,000 United States service personnel died during the conflict. However, President Johnson did not have to resign or suffer any consequences for his actions even though the Gulf of Tonkin myth had been exposed as early as 1964. Daniel Ellsberg, who was on duty in the Pentagon on the night of August 4 receiving messages from the USS Maddox, reported that the ship was on a secret electronic warfare support measures mission (code-named DESOTO) near Northern Vietnamese territorial waters. He was later to figure in the infamous leak of the Pentagon Papers from the Brooklyn Institute and the raid by FBI and CIA agents on his psychiatrist's office that was attributed to President Nixon.

Since 1961, the USS Maddox and other US warships had been provoking retaliatory actions from the North Vietnamese for months according to Operation Plan 34-alpha. President Johnson survived unscathed as there was no media campaign against him. However, he did not stand for re-election in 1968 as the stress of the war was too great for him to handle. As a result, President Nixon was elected on a ticket to withdraw from Vietnam by implementing the policy of Peace with Honour.

2. Ngo Dinh Diem was the Catholic president of the mainly Buddhist South Vietnam. When Ngo failed to obtain support from his people, he was killed in a coup by his generals led by Big Minh, with the tacit approval of the American administration of John F Kennedy in 1963, and the Central Intelligence Agency (CIA). President John F Kennedy had changed his mind about supporting Ngo and was on the point of withdrawing the military advisors from South Vietnam, when he was assassinated in Dallas and replaced by President Johnson. Ngo was a bright lad in his youth. He was reputed to be the headmaster of a school by the age of twenty-two. The former Emperor Bao Dai of Vietnam appointed him as the Prime Minister of the state of Vietnam. At that time Vietnam had already been partitioned at the Geneva Conference held in 1954. The Geneva Accord, however, was not signed by the US government or the government of South Vietnam. Using that excuse, Ngo refused to hold the re-unification elections that were part of the provisions of the Geneva Accord. Instead he organized a referendum in October 1955 on whether South Vietnam should become a republic. Ngo won the referendum. It was alleged that the referendum was rigged by his brother. After winning the referendum, Ngo Dinh Diem proclaimed himself the President of the newly created Republic of Vietnam. The two brothers escaped to the Chinese district of Cholon after the military coup in 1963. However, they were re-captured

and killed by men of General Big Minh. They were on their way to Tan Son Nhut Airport where they were supposed to be flown to a safe haven. They had to be killed as the conspirators feared a political comeback by the resourceful brothers. President Kennedy was reported to be shocked when he heard the news that the Ngo brothers had been killed. Their assassination was not supposed to be part of the plan. Cable 243 was also known as DEPTEL 243 or Telegram 243. This was the high-profile telegram sent by the US Department of State to Ambassador Henry Cabot Lodge in Saigon on the night of August 24, 1963. There had been allegations that these cables were forgeries by Howard Hunt and associates, on behalf of Nixon. However, the fact that Ngo Dinh Diem was overthrown with the consent and approval of the US government had never been disputed. Several nights previously, the Ngo brothers had organized a raid on Buddhist temples and killed several hundred monks, exacerbating the Catholic/Buddhist divide of the country. The cable represented a change from the US policy of support for Ngo Dinh Diem and his brother. It authorized Henry Cabot Lodge to give the green light to the generals of the Army of the Republic of Vietnam (ARVN), led by General Big Minh, to mount a coup that would result in the death of the Ngo brothers.

3. Iran-Contra, also known as Irangate, was the scandal during Reagan's tenure in the 1980s as the President of the United States. During the Reagan's presidency, senior officials in his administration had secretly facilitated the sale of arms to Iran, through Israel. Iran at the time was officially subjected to an US arms embargo, following the hostage-

taking of personnel of the US Embassy in Teheran during President Carter's administration, some years previously. The United States was also officially on the side of Iraq during the Iran-Iraq War. Some US officials also hoped that the money from the arms sales could be used to secure the release of the hostages and at the same time also allow US intelligence agencies to fund the Nicaraguan Contras. Under the Boland Amendment, further funding of the Contras by the US government had been prohibited by Congress. The Nicaraguan Contras were a guerrilla group funded and supported by the United States to oppose the democratically elected socialist government of the Sandinistas of Nicaragua, which was perceived to be anti-US. The modus operandi of the Contras was terror, by killing and maiming innocent women and children in violation of human rights. To this day, it is unclear exactly what Reagan, who supported the Contras, knew and when, and whether the arms sales were motivated by his desire to save the US hostages. After the weapon sales were revealed in November 1986, Reagan appeared on national television and stated that the weapons transfers had indeed occurred, but that the United States did not trade arms for hostages. At the hearings of the Tower Commission appointed by President Reagan, Reagan famously declared that he had forgotten what had actually happened. Unlike Nixon, Reagan was not hounded personally by a hostile press. This was despite the fact that the Irangate scandal could be classed as much more serious than Watergate, as it involved foreign countries and also broke the rules of an arms embargo that was supposed to be official United States policy. The media accepted Reagan's explanation that what had started as an initiative to open relations with Iran had in its implementation deteriorated into an arms exchange for the release of hostages. Several high officials were indicted, including Secretary of Defense, Casper Weinberger and Admiral Poindexter. However, they were given presidential pardons by President George Bush senior who was the Vice-President in the Reagan administration.

4 Yellowcake. This was the myth generated by the Italian Intelligence Agency and then the British government under Tony Blair that Saddam Hussein was buying five hundred tons of yellowcake or uranium concentrate from Niger. It was to be one of the 'proofs' that Saddam was out to create a nuclear bomb and weapons of mass destruction (WMD), and Iraq should therefore be invaded to ensure the safety of the rest of the free world. Scooter Libby, the Chief of Staff of Vice-President Dick Cheney, released the name of Valarie Plame Wilson, an active CIA operative, to the press as an act of revenge against Joe Wilson, ex-ambassador to Niger. He was the husband of Valarie Wilson and had been to Niger on a CIA mission to verify the story. Wilson had returned, saying that it was impossible that Saddam was buying yellowcake from Niger. Despite Joe Wilson's negative conclusion, President Bush used the yellowcake myth at his State of the Union speech to justify the invasion of Iraq. Wilson had then written and published an account in *The New York Times*, refuting the President. The Wilsons had to be punished for opposing the policy of the White House. Their story had been made into a film in 2010, called *Fair Game*, starring Sean Penn and Naomi Watts. Vice-President Dick Cheney

escaped unscathed. Scooter Libby his Chief of Staff had to resign. He was indicted in 2005 for releasing the name of Valarie Plame Wilson to the press as an active CIA operative. He thus became the fall guy for his boss. His thirty-month sentence was later commuted by President GW Bush.

5. Weapons of Mass Destruction (WMD). This was the excuse used by US President George W Bush and British Prime Minister Tony Blair to justify the 'shock and awe' invasion of Saddam Hussein's Iraq. Among the manufactured evidence were the 'aluminium tubes' and yellowcake myths, generated to paint Saddam Hussein as the dictator that had to be deposed when it was clear that his nuclear programme had been destroyed during the first Iraq War in 1991. Exposure of the myth had resulted in the death, in rather mysterious circumstances, of David Kelly, a senior weapons inspector working for the British government. Why was there a need to get rid of Saddam Hussein? Various hypotheses have been generated and the one that makes most sense was the attempt by Saddam Hussein to sell Iraqi oil for Euros. His bluster had been echoed by Iran and North Korea – the so-called axis of evil. Traditionally, all trade in oil had been conducted in US dollars. As all oil transactions had hitherto to be paid for in US dollars, any country needing to buy oil had to buy US dollars. This fact alone had maintained the status of the US dollar as the world's fait reserve currency despite its break from the gold standard in 1971. Saddam's action, if allowed to continue, would break the US monopoly in the oil trade and could jeopardize the supremacy of the US dollar. This hypothesis is strengthened by the fact that both France and Germany were against the attack on

Saddam Hussein's Iraq initially and suffered the wrath of the United States. France was labeled as the Surrender Monkeys and French fries in the United States were renamed 'freedom fries'. The initial code name for the Iraq War was Operation Iraq Liberation which would have the acronym of OIL. It was therefore renamed Operation Iraq Freedom. Following the invasion, the US-led Iraq Survey Group concluded that Iraq had indeed ended its nuclear, chemical, and biological programmes in 1991, some ten years previously. The finding of the absence of WMD was too late, as Baghdad had been destroyed and hundreds of thousands of innocent Iraqis had paid for the regime change with their lives.

6. Memes. Richard Dawkins in his seminal tome *The Selfish Gene*, published in 1976, first gave birth to the term 'meme', shortened from the ancient Greek word 'mimeme', meaning 'something imitated'. By meme, Dawkins means that ideas, like genes, can take on a life of their own. Thus, memes can self-replicate, mutate and respond to selective pressures. To illustrate this, he uses the example of jokes that seem to be able to circumnavigate the world several times at what seems to be lightning speed when they are especially apt, even though the original authors remain unknown. He posits that memes, like genes, are in constant battle for survival, and only the best memes (ideas/jokes/melodies) would survive the competition for attention. Meme is Dawkins' hypothesis and explanation on how cultural ideas may spread from one mind to another and evolve.

7. The Watergate arrests. Watergate raiders were arrested at their third attempt. This is not a well-known fact. (See p. 5,

para 5 in *Watergate: The Corruption of American Politics and the Fall of Richard Nixon.* by Fred Emery. It is not been well publicized that the Watergate arrests of the five culprits was at their third attempt at breaking into the offices of the Democratic National Committee at Watergate. This, together with the evidence that the money found on the Cuban ex-CIA operatives had consecutive serial numbers and that Howard Hunt's name and details were conveniently to be found in the address books of two of the arrested Cubans, suggest that the Watergate arrests were in fact a set-up rather than the commonly acknowledged cock-up. Howard Hunt's name led to the involvement of the White House that generated the media hysteria that led ultimately to Nixon's resignation from the Presidency of the United States. The serially numbered notes were used to trace the slush fund, laundered in Mexico and controlled by Maurice Stans, a Nixon's man tasked with coordinating the finances of the Committee to Re-elect the President (CRP). The Watergate break in was the idea of Gordon Liddy who was an advisor to CRP, misnamed as CREEP by the media. He had earlier master-minded the break in to Daniel Ellsberg's psychiatrist, Dr Fielding, to obtain evidence for the leaking of the Pentagon Papers. A full account of the Watergate raids and arrests which led to the fall of the Nixon White House has been documented in Fred Emery's book. The author describes the raids as 'hilarious'. The raids were so badly organized that one wonders if they were carried out to court arrest and to plant evidence in the direction of the Nixon White House.

Chapter 1 - Ping Pong Diplomacy

1. The World Table Tennis Championship has been held every two years since 1926 when it was first held in London. At the beginning, Hungarian players were the force to be reckoned with. However, since 1960, China regularly has the best players in the world. In 1971, the Championship was held in Nagoya.

2. Glenn Cowan was born in 1952 and was nineteen years of age when he and Zhuang Zedong began the ping pong diplomacy. He died in 2004 after a coronary artery by-pass operation. Zhuang Zedong expressed his greatest regrets in not seeing Glenn again after the meeting in Nagoya. He did visit Glenn's mother in 2007 in the USA.

3. Zhuang Zedong, a Chinese table tennis player and three times world champion, in 1961, 1963 and 1965. Together with Glenn Cowan he made history when they met in Nagoya, Japan and began what has become known as the ping pong diplomacy. It is not known how much of the meeting had been pre-choreographed.

4. Chinese table tennis players. The Chinese players have replaced the Hungarians as the best players in the world. Some of them have a most intriguing way of serving the ping pong ball. They toss the ball several meters into the air before hitting the ball low across the table. Cowan, like many table tennis aficionados across the world, had never seen anything like this before and thought it was most awesome. He made a mental note that it was a technique he needed to practice and perfect. By tossing the ball high into the air, one could disguise the serve, varying it from a

glancing serve to a top-spin serve or a smashing serve. As the ping pong ball travels at great speed, it confers a great advantage to be able to disguise the serve, as it gives the opponent a little less time to read the ball's trajectory and respond. The millisecond difference can make a huge difference between winning and losing a service game.

5. Huangshan or Yellow Mountain is famed for its beauty. It was the subject of the silk screen picture that Zhuang Zedong gave to Glenn Cowan at the opening of the ping pong diplomacy in Japan.

6. Chairman Mao or Mao Zedong was the revolutionary leader who led the Communist Party of China and the Chinese people in its national liberation war against Japan and then against the Guomindang government of Chiang Kai-shek. Mao declared the founding of the People's Republic of China on October 1, 1949 when he announced that the Chinese people had stood up. Lin Biao was a highly talented general during the national liberation wars and was directly responsible for the liberation of the north-east China. In 1966 he was made the Vice-Chairman of the People's Republic of China, effectively the heir to Mao. However, there were important policy differences between the two on the economy and also in assessing the danger that the Soviet Union posed to China. It has been reported that Lin Biao was opposed to the rapprochement with the USA and Nixon's visit. He formed Project 571 whose purpose was to mount a coup d'état against Mao. When the plot failed, he tried to flee to the Soviet Union in a Tri-Star. The airplane crashed in Outer Mongolia, killing him. Deshpande,

GP, 'Fall of Lin Biao' *Economic and Political Weekly*, 7 (1972): 1501-1052 gives a full account of the plot.

7. Dr Norman Bethune was a member of the Communist Party of Canada and a Canadian surgeon who was attached to the Eighth Route Army that fought the Japanese forces occupying northern China at the time. He developed septicaemia from a needle stick injury while operating on injured comrade soldiers. He died from the septicaemia in 1939. Mao wrote an article entitled *In Memory of Norman Bethune*.

Chapter 2 - The China Lobby

1. Flying Tigers. The Flying Tigers of the US Air Force supported the Chindits, the name given to the group of British soldiers under the command of Major General Orde Charles Wingate who threatened the Japanese army in Burma. The Flying Tigers flew sorties over the hump from Burma into Chongqing, China to support the war effort there. The Nationalist government of Chiang Kai-shek had established Chongqing as its wartime capital, having lost both Beijing and Nanjing to the Japanese. General Stilwell was the commander of the Chinese Army in India (CAI). He commanded the CAI as though it were an American unit and had a very aggressive policy towards the Japanese army. He was reassigned in 1944 after falling out with Generalissimo Chiang Kai-shek. He had disagreements with Chiang over the strategic purpose of weapons sent by the government of the United States of America. General Vinegar Joe Stilwell wanted to use the weapons to fight the Japanese while

Chiang wanted to keep the weapons for the fight against Mao's forces after the expected defeat of Japan.

2. Song Meiling. She was the ravishingly beautiful and youngest of the three Song girls of the patriotic Chinese Minister Charlie Song. She married Chiang Kai-shek and with the eldest sister, Ailing were part of the ruling clique in Guomindang China. Ailing was married to the richest man in China at the time – HH Kong who was to be the Finance Minister in Chiang Kai-shek's nationalist government. The second sister, Qingling, married Sun Yat-sen and remained in China and was, with Dong Biwu, one of two Vice-Chairpersons of the People's Republic of China from 1959. Like the country, the Song family was split along the lines of the Communist Party and the Nationalist Guomindang. Qingling, by remaining in China, lent legitimacy to the Communist Party as the heir to alliance with the Guomindang of Sun Yat-sen's, an alliance which he had actively fostered.

3. General Stilwell. There is a memorial to General Stilwell near the city of Chongqing as he is considered to be a friend of the Chinese people.

4. CHRD. There are many types of Council for Human Rights and Democracy. There is one in the United Nations, and also in many countries, in both the developed and developing world. There is the European Commission for Human Rights. Libya and Egypt, after the Arab Spring, now have Human Rights and Democracy Councils. It is not known how many of

these councils are front organizations of the United States or the United Kingdom.

5. Guomindang. This was the party that was founded by Sun Yat-sen to overthrow the Manchu dynasty that had failed China in the late eighteenth and early nineteenth century. Sun Yat-sen led the party into an alliance with the Communist Party of China. After overthrowing the Manchu dynasty, Dr Sun abdicated the presidency in favor of Yuan Shikai, who led a short period of restoration by crowning himself the emperor of China. Dr Sun died from liver cancer in 1924 and his position was usurped by Generalissimo Chiang Kai-shek, who reneged on the Communists, killing thousands of patriotic Chinese Communists during the Northern Expedition of 1927. The Guomindang under Chiang Kai-shek, lost China to the much better organized and non-corrupt communist People's Liberation Army. He fled to Taiwan in 1949, creating the Republic of China there, which occupied China's seat on the Security Council of the United Nations. It was voted out in 1971 and the rightful place returned to the People's Republic of China with a population of 1.64 billion; people who had all this time been disenfranchised in the leading body of the world's nations.

6. Zionist Israel is the homeland given to the Zionist Jews by the British under the Balfour Treaty. The Zionist state of Israel was established in 1948 after a campaign of terror when British and Arab nationals were bombed into submission. Millions of Arabs left Palestine to become a diaspora of refugees. The Jews of the Zionist state have to be differentiated from non-Zionist Jews who oppose the

way the state of Israel has been established over Arab lands. It is said that Zionist Israel is the US fifth column in the Middle East in order that the United States may have control over an oil-rich region of the world.

7. Templar Knights. The Templar Knights have their origins from the medieval days when they were warriors, diplomats, bankers, builders, farmers, engineers, monks, protectors of pilgrims and more. The Order of the Templar Knights was founded by Hugh de Payens in 1119 in Jerusalem. The very wealthy medieval organization had many enemies and fell into disrepute throughout Europe after suffering persecution by Pope Clements V; its Grand Master was burnt at the stake in Paris in 1314. The modern Templar Knights was founded in Paris in 1804. It is a right wing Christian organization, with international links. The Knights Templar International has a branch even in the United Nations.

8. Edgar Snow is the famed author of the book *Red Star over China*, published in 1936 – the first ever account by a western journalist of the Chinese Communists who were based in Yan'an and fighting against the Japanese invaders. It has been said that his book on the Chinese Revolution is equivalent to John Reed's *Ten Days that Shook the World*, the classic account of the Russian October Revolution of 1917. Since those early days, Edgar Snow had been a friend of the Chinese people. The Chinese leaders with his permission, made use of his friendship to make pronouncements on world affairs. It was therefore of great significance that he was seen with Mao on Tian'an Gate in 1970 for the celebrations to commemorate the founding of the People's

Republic. It was a signal by Mao that a new era of rapprochement with the United States was at hand.

9. The Bombing of Hanoi. This took place at Christmas 1972, after Nixon had been re-elected. Nixon had a policy of withdrawing from Vietnam but only on the basis of Peace with Honour, despite knowing that the United States could never win a non-nuclear land war against the Vietnamese Communists. When the secret talks in Paris had stalled, because of obstruction by President Thieu of South Vietnam, Nixon wrongly believed that he could bomb the Vietnamese back to the negotiating table. Using the provisions handed by Congress after the Gulf of Tonkin Incident, he began a campaign to bomb Hanoi during the Christmas of 1972, using B52 stratobombers. The largest tonnage of bombs (20,237 tons in total) since the Second World War was unleashed on Hanoi in the eleven days of bombing, December 18 to 29. There were at least 1,600 Vietnamese civilians killed. Of the 741 sorties by the B52 bombers the North Vietnamese claimed to have shot down thirty-four B52s and four F-111 fighter bombers.

10. The Kent State University shooting of several innocent university students by the Ohio National Guardsmen on May 4, 1970 was the direct result of Nixon and Kissinger's escalation of the Vietnam War into Cambodia at Parrot's Beak. After the invasion, there were student demonstrations across the entire country to express their outrage at what was being done in their name. It was at one of these demonstrations at Kent State University when four students, who were not even demonstrating, were shot dead and nine

injured. It was the first time that young Americans had been killed by US servicemen in USA and the repressive nature of the American state was exposed. The anger felt across the country was palpable and resulted in a strike by over four million college students throughout the country. It was also the backdrop to President Nixon's visit one night to the Lincoln Memorial to meet the students, accompanied only by his butler.

11. RAND Corporation is a United States think-tank formed to offer research and analysis to the United States armed forces and was funded initially by Douglas Aircraft Company. It is currently financed by the US government. It has four major sites in the US and also offices in the UK, Belgium, Qatar, Abu Dhabi in the United Arab Emirates and Mexico. Since the 1950s it has defined US military strategy. The Mutual Assured Destruction (MAD) and the game theories of war were the brain children of RAND. The infamous Herman Kahn developed the idea of a winnable nuclear war in his book On Thermonuclear War. He was satirized in the film Dr Strangelove. In this light it is interesting to note that the People's Republic of China is the only nuclear power that has declared a non-first use of nuclear weapons, which is that China's nuclear weapons are purely for defense.

Chapter 3 - The Plot

1. Military Industrial Complex (MIC). This was the term used to by President Eisenhower in his presidential farewell speech. He warned the United States and the people of the world of the tremendous power and reach of the Military

Industrial Complex. The term is now used to cover the network of contracts, and the flow of money to individuals and organizations of defense contractors, the Pentagon, Congress and the Executive Branch. Cases of political corruption in these organizations have surfaced with regularity. The MIC exists not only in the United States but in many developed countries, such as the UK, France and Germany where such an infrastructure exists to serve the military and defense industries.

2. 1984. This is the title of a novel by George Orwell in which he gives a fictionalized account of a state in the future in which the citizens are monitored and programmed to do things against their wishes. It has been hailed as the model of what dictatorship in the future would be like. It has also been used to describe a communist society.

Chapter 4 - The Nixon Plan

1. *Nuclear Weapons and Foreign Policy*. Written by Henry Kissinger in 1957, the book examines the changes in geopolitics that are a consequence of nuclear weapons. He concludes that nuclear weapons are useless as adjuncts to foreign policy due to their lack of credibility. He favours beefing up the conventional military weapon systems to project the military might of the United States.

2. The Korean War happened in the 1950s. North Korea had launched an invasion against the south and had driven the US troops back before the US launched a counter-offensive that drove the North Korean forces to its border with China at the Yalu River. At the Potsdam Conference, the allies had

unilaterally divided Korea without consulting the Korean people. General MacArthur had wanted to use nuclear bombs against the Chinese but was overruled and then sacked by President Truman. The US was able to assemble a United Nations force due to the absence of the Soviet delegation at the crucial Security Council meeting. The Chinese volunteers, under the command of Marshall Peng Dehuai, drove the US troops back to the 38th parallel and then withdrew unilaterally and unconditionally. There have been speculations that the Chinese were forced into this unwanted war by Kim Il Sung with Stalin's backing. It is said that Stalin had wanted both the Chinese and US armies to be exhausted. An armistice was eventually declared and the shooting stopped in 1953. The Korean Peninsula is still divided, with the south under US tutelage.

3. Henry Kissinger was a German professor of political science at Harvard University before his appointment in 1968 to be the Advisor to the National Security Agency (NSA). It has been said that his appointment had been one of the first acts of President Nixon after his inauguration as the thirty-seventh President of the United States. He outlived Nixon. He had written many books including The White House Years.

4. Twenty-seven Soviet Divisions. The conflict between the Soviet Union and China began as ideological differences on how to interpret Stalin's place in history. Some authorities have maintained that Mao had smarted under the Soviet's big brother behaviour and wanted to be treated with equality. When in 1960 Khrushchev unilaterally withdrew

Soviet experts from all over China, he also amassed some twenty-seven divisions of Soviet troops along their common border. The fear of an attack by the Soviet Union is believed to be the reason why Mao's China was receptive to Nixon's overture.

5. Pearl S Buck. She was an American writer whose parents were Presbyterian missionaries and had lived in China until 1934. Her novel The *Good Earth* won the Pulitzer Prize in 1932 and she was the first American woman to be awarded the Nobel Prize for Literature in 1938. She was famous for translating the Chinese classic *Outlaws of the Marshes* which she entitled *All Men are Brothers*. It has been said that she was instrumental in the love affair between the American and Chinese peoples through her books on China's peasantry.

6. France and the gold standard. Due to the Vietnam War and other conflicts after the Second World War, although the United States at Bretton Woods had successfully deposed and replaced Great Britain's pound sterling with the US dollar as the world's reserve currency, by the 1970s, the US economy was in trouble. There were very much more US dollars in circulation than there were gold in Fort Knox. France was one of the countries holding large reserves of US dollars. De Gaulle, always with France's interest at heart, wanted to replace the US dollar with the French franc as the global reserve currency. He devised the scheme of demanding that the United States repaid French-held dollars with gold bullion. He led a multitude of countries in this demand, which placed tremendous pressure on the US

financial system. However, Nixon, together with John Connolly, the Democratic Secretary of the Treasury, broke the link of the dollar with gold and in a thrice solved the problem of solvency of the US dollar. The US dollar has remained the world's fait reserve currency till today. All transactions in oil have to be paid for in dollars, forcing any country which needs oil to buy US dollar bills. As the US dollar is the world's reserve currency, whenever the US government needs more dollars, all it has to do is to print more dollars. It is as if money can be conjured from thin air. It is this facility that has been blamed for today's global economic woes.

7. Lend-Lease Loans. It was the programme by which the US supplied the allies – Great Britain, France, Russia, China – and other allied nations with war material during the Second World War. Great Britain had to borrow from the United States of America $31 billion (1941 value) worth of war material and foodstuffs in order to be able to fight Nazi Germany. The material was shipped from the US to Great Britain by Atlantic convoys that were attacked by Germany's wolf pack submarines. After the war, James Callaghan, future British Prime Minister, was part of a mission to the US to re-negotiate the terms of the loan, which was refused. The size of the loans was instrumental in the US dollar displacing the pound sterling as the world's reserve currency. Great Britain has been subservient to the US ever since. This is why the so-called 'Special Relationship' is so important to the British. The Lend-Lease loan was finally paid off on December 29, 2006 by a payment of $83.3 million. Ed Balls, the then Treasury Secretary, formally gave

thanks to the US government for their support at the time of Great Britain's need.

8. The Shanghai Communique. This was drafted during Nixon's visit to China in 1972. The principles of the communique were agreed during Kissinger's preliminary trip to meet with Zhou Enlai. Zhou did not want a bland document covered with diplomat niceties but without any substance. It was agreed the two sides would first set down their differences before setting out the common grounds. There was a last-minute problem with the wording with regard to Taiwan. The sticking point was the withdrawal of US forces from Taiwan. A compromise was eventually reached in which no time scale was set for the withdrawal of U S forces from Taiwan.

Chapter 5 - Nixon Visits China

1. The book by Margaret MacMillan entitled *Seize the Hour: When Nixon met Mao* is a good resource book for this chapter. There is much background information. It is well written and reads like a novel.

2. 'Chinese and dogs are not allowed'. Humiliating notices declaring that Chinese and dogs were not allowed in the parks of Shanghai because they were reserved for the use of foreigners infuriated the Chinese nation. It was therefore unsurprising that the Communist Party of China could call upon a great deal of support from among the patriotic Chinese nationals. All Chinese felt a sense of pride when Mao declared in October 1949 that 'The Chinese had stood

up and that no nation will be able to humiliate the Chinese people ever again'.

3. Zhou's handshake snub. The 1954 Geneva Conference was held to discuss and sign the Geneva Accords on Vietnam after the defeat of France at Dien Bien Phu in 1952 by the Vietnamese led by General Giap. John Foster Dulles, the then Secretary of State for the United States, refused to shake the hand of Chinese Premier Zhou Enlai. He also made sure that none of his subordinates shook the hands of their Chinese counterparts. The US delegation refused to sign the Geneva Accords and later used that as the reason to intervene in Vietnam and to start the US War in Vietnam.

4. Prince Norodom Sihanouk was the last king of Cambodia. He had the reputation as a survivor against all the odds. He was deposed by a US-backed military coup led by Lon Nol in 1970. He exiled himself to Beijing, where he was awarded the trappings of a king in exile. Sihanouk supported the Khmer Rouge's attempt to overthrow Lon Nol who turned out to be a puppet of the US. He eventually was deposed by the Vietnamese invasion of Cambodia.

Chapter 6 - Preparing the Trap

1. Pentagon Papers. These were highly sensitive and secret documents of the US government that were leaked by Daniel Ellsberg, a disillusioned Vietnam veteran who was working at the liberal think-tank – the Brookings Institute. Nixon initially thought the Pentagon Papers would be politically advantageous to him as they revealed the machinations of the Democratic presidencies of the recent

past. However, when the leaks turned into a flood and began to embarrass the US government, he changed his mind and decided to prosecute those responsible for the leaks. The White House 'plumbers' were formed in an attempt to stem the leakage of sensitive government documents, as Nixon could not get the FBI or the CIA to cooperate.

2. EOB Office. When the Nixons first moved into the White House, Pat Nixon made alterations to the Oval Office. She warmed it with a rich blue and gold rug and gold-coloured sofas and curtains. Nixon felt that it was too formal. He had the office at the Executive Office Building next to the White House redecorated for his use. He had it decorated with momentos that he had acquired over the years. There were many photographs of the family. There was a photo of Pat, Tricia, Julie and Nixon taken in California on the day they had moved back after losing the 1960 election to John Kennedy. The shelves were filled with Nixon's favourite books. Nixon preferred to work and think in this office surround by his personal possessions rather than in the more formal Oval Office.

3. Chappaquiddick. On July 19, 1969, Edward Kennedy was alleged to have driven his car off a quay into a tidal channel. Mary Jo Kopichne, a young lady was found dead beneath the car. After pleading guilty to the charge of leaving the scene of an accident, Ted Kennedy went to jail for two months. The incident was a national scandal and could be the reason why Ted Kennedy did not run for the presidency of the United States in 1972 and 1976.

Chapter 8 - Springing the Trap

1. Watergate break in. *Watergate: The Corruption of American Politics and the Fall of Richard Nixon* by Fred Emery is a very detailed source of information about what happened during the Watergate break in. It contains a great deal of facts but little analysis. It adopts the conventional story of a cover-up etc. and describes the Watergate break in as 'hilarious'. It never explored the possibility that the entire saga was a setup.

Chapter 9 - Sarah Cornfield

1. 'Puff the Magic Dragon'. Not many of those who lived in the sixties, but were not involved in the drug scene, knew what the song alludes to. In fact it is a reference to the smoking of pot hence 'Puff the Magic Dragon'.

2. Franz Fanon is the author of *The Wretched of the Earth*, an account of the Algerian struggle for liberation from the French colonizers. It is his most famous work written in French. As a psychiatrist, he explores the effect of colonization upon the psyche of a nation. In the 1960s it was a required reading of the New Left.

3. Marcuse. Herbert Marcuse was a professor at the University of California, Berkeley. His claims to fame are his books *Eros and Civilization* and *The One Dimensional Man*. He was willing to speak at student teach-ins and was thus known as the father of the New Left in America. He was known to have influenced activists such as Angela Davis and

Rudi Dutschke. He was criticized by Marxist writers such as Paul Mattick.

4. Students for Democratic Society (SDS). The SDS was a radical student movement in vogue at the height of the opposition to the Vietnam War in the United States of America in the 1960s. Part of it evolved into the Weathermen, a terrorist organization. Tom Haydon was one of its leaders. During President Johnson's escalation of the Vietnam War in 1965, the SDS organized student revolts throughout the campuses of the United States, starting in the University of Michigan, which held the first anti-war teach-in. The slogan 'If you are not part of the solution you are part of the problem', is believed to have been coined by a SDS activist. However, the lack of ideological leadership led to the movement's degeneration.

Chapter 10 - The Assignment

1. *The Washington Post*. This national daily carried the first of many accounts of the Watergate break in. The two young reporters Bob Woodward and Carl Bernstein have written two books giving accounts of their work in unraveling the mysteries of Watergate. The two books are *All the President's Men* and *The Final Days*. The former has been made into a film classic, starring Robert Redford and Dustin Hoffman. Both books have been criticized for having many facts that are jumbled and rather incoherent. More serious is the recent criticism that some of the accounts in the book are fictitious. It has been said that there was no way that anyone could see the flower pot placed by the window from the

road which, according to the book, was a signal to Deep Throat that Bob Woodward needed help. It is also questioned that, as the newspapers were delivered in a pile rather than individually to the apartments, it would be extremely difficult and laborious to leave messages to meet on the crossword puzzle page of the papers. In *All the President's Men* it is said that Deep Throat would draw a picture of a clock-face with its hands pointing to the time to meet. Although Carl Bernstein has not been heard of much more, Bob Woodward has gone on to write books about the George W Bush's White House and the preparation for the Iraq War. A recent biography by Himmelman of Ben Bradlee the editor of *The Washington Post* of the time , questions the veracity of the accounts about 'Deep Throat' and described Ben Bradlee's concerns expressed in an interview. There was also a 7 page memorandum that was supposed to be written by Carl Bernstein after he had <u>illegally</u> interviewed a member of the Grand Jury associated with Watergate.

Chapter 12 - Lucky Break

1. 'Bridge over Troubled Waters'. This was a hit pop song of the seventies. The single was released on January 26, 1970. It was written by Paul Simon and sung by Art Garfunkel. The song almost defined the era and is believed to have led to the break-up of the duo.

2. Deep Throat was the name given by *The Washington Post* to their Watergate deep cover source. It should not be confused with the pornographic book and film around that time. Until May 31, 2005 when Mark Felt declared that he

was the Deep Throat of Watergate fame, Deep Throat had remained for years as one of the famous US mysteries. Mark Felt was in his nineties at the time of his revelation and died a couple of years later. It has been assumed that he became Deep Throat out of spite at having been passed over for the position of the as director of the FBI after Edgar Hoover's death. He had been Edgar's deputy for more than thirty years. It was Patrick Gray, Nixon's political appointee, who was made the FBI director. Before Mark Felt's disclosure, various names had been on the suspect lists. They included General Al Haig and John Dean.

Chapter 13 - Sarah Meets Nixon

1. Meeting Nixon. Some readers may say that the way Sarah met Nixon is not plausible. They should remember that Nixon had a very impulsive nature. This was exemplified by his visit, late one night, accompanied only by his butler, to the students who were at the Lincoln Memorial demonstrating about the Kent State University killings. Given Nixon's personality and the siege mentality at the White House at the time, it is not implausible that such a meeting could take place.

Nixon – A Brief Biography

1. Richard Milhous Nixon. Good accounts of Nixon the man can be gleaned from reading his books *Six Crises* and *RN: The Memoirs of Richard Nixon*.

2. Algers Hiss. Nixon in his capacity as a member of the US Congress and the Committee of Un-American Activities was

instrumental in exposing Alger Hiss as a the communist mole just after the Second World War. By so doing, he made many enemies who were to plague him in his later political career. His enemies were mainly journalists and editors of liberal newspapers such as Ben Bradlee of *The Washington Post*. They were friends of Algers Hiss and never suspected his role as the deep communist mole and wrote extensively in support of him. Nixon was not the right wing ogre that he was painted to be. Although a member of the Republican Party, he was mainly a patriot and motivated by a sense to do whatever was necessary to keep the United States strong. He was a foreign policy expert and had written extensively on the shifting power between China and the Soviet Union.

3. Senator Joe McCarthy. Many casual followers of American politics mix up the timings of Senator McCarthy's right wing radicalism (1950s) with that of Nixon (1948). In fact his unsavoury activities, known now as McCarthyism, in the Committee of Un-American Activities took place <u>after</u> Nixon had left the Committee to be a senator. It could be said that McCarthy's activities in the Committee was an attempt to emulate the stellar political rise of Richard Nixon. Nixon was motivated to ensure that fair play was done in the work of the Committee. In that sense he was quite the opposite of McCarthy, although a reading of the press of that time would suggest otherwise.

4. President Dwight Eisenhower, who was the thirty-fourth President of the United States and a kind of elder statesman, had pointed out the dangers of the Military Industrial Complex In his farewell speech before his 'retirement' from

presidential politics. He warned of the runaway military spending of the United States and its ubiquitous and pernicious influence on all aspects of policy-making in the United States. The Military Industrial Complex is a concept that is used to refer to the policy and monetary relationship between the members of the national arms forces, the industry and legislators. The relations include the all-important political contributions that sustain political campaigns, defense spending and political lobbies to support and influence the decision-making bureaucracies and legislatures. Although first described in the United States, the Military Industrial Complex is found in any advanced country, such as Great Britain, France and Germany. It can also be defined as an informal and changing coalition of groups with vested psychological, moral, and material interests in the continuous development and maintenance of high levels of weaponry, in the preservation of colonial markets and in military-strategic conceptions of internal affairs. Currently, the United States spends nearly 50 per cent of the entire world's expenditure on the military and armaments. One can reasonably ask why such large expenditures?

5. *Team of Rivals* is the book written by Doris Kearns Goodwin about President Lincoln's uncanny ability to bring in leaders from opposing camps into his government. It was touted as the way President Obama would be working after his election to the US Presidency.   Nixon was a superb practitioner of the same policy as long ago as the late 1960s. He had John Connolly, a Democrat to be his Treasury Secretary and also appointed Henry Kissinger, who for years

had been the foreign policy advisor to Nelson Rockefeller, Nixon's Republican rival, to be the National Security Agency Advisor and then as the Secretary of State.

6. John Connolly. He was a Democrat but was appointed by Nixon to be his Treasury Secretary. He was with President JF Kennedy when the latter was shot in the head driving through downtown Dallas.

7. SALT. The Strategic Arms Limitation Talks was the joint policy of President Nixon and Henry Kissinger. On geopolitics, they had both come to the conclusion that Russia and China were not a single bloc and that the new development of nuclear arms by the Soviet Union would threaten US hegemony. Nixon sent Kissinger to pave the way for the SALT talks that were conducted in Moscow. Nixon's stated motivation was to avoid a nuclear world war and to establish a peaceful world for all children, his and others.

8. War in East Pakistan (Bangladesh). The 1970 Pakistani elections ignited the Bangladesh Liberation War. The Awami League had won 167 of the 169 seats and secured an overwhelming majority in the Pakistan Parliament. General Yahya Khan lost the war to the Bangladeshi forces supported by the Indian army. The Awami League leader Sheikh Mujibur Rahman became the President of Bangladesh after the war.

There were reports that the East Pakistan army committed many atrocities and that Nixon had ignored them. Before heaping blame on Nixon for his failure to intervene, it must be remembered that at that time Pakistan was a major conduit of messages to China and crucial to the success of Nixon's foreign policy initiative with China.

9. The gold standard. Up until 1971, the American dollar had been linked to the gold held in Fort Knox, with one ounce of gold being equivalent to US$35. With the large sums of money spent to fight the US War in Vietnam, France, leading many other countries, campaigned for gold in exchange for the large sums of dollars held in reserve by other countries. Nixon in 1971 made a decisive break of the dollar from gold and in a thrice got America out of a sticky situation. There are economic and political observers who place the present economic crisis firmly on Nixon's decision to break the link between the US dollar and gold. Nixon's supporters would say that his action enabled politicians to provide American citizens of at least two generations with an excellent standard of living. Opponents of the policy of quantity easing, such as the Austrian school of economists, claim that throughout the years, in particular the past few years, the US Federal Reserve has been printing dollars (quantity easing) to keep the US economy afloat. They believe that a problem caused by massive debts cannot be salvaged by generating more debts. As a simple example they point to the deteriorating value of the dollar relative to gold. When the gold standard was first established, US$35 would buy one ounce of gold. The cost of one ounce of gold is now more than US$1,500. The cost of one ounce of gold is expected to range between US$3,000 and US$4,000 by the end of 2012 to reflect the massive debt that the US has generated by the

process of printing money out of thin air. At some point in time the paper dollar has to be paid for.

10. The Yom Kippur War which was started by the Egyptians in October 1973 was an attempt by the Egyptians and Syrians to regain the territories from Israel lost during the Six Day War of 1967. The Egyptians attacked across the Suez Canal, surprising the Israeli. Israel was able to wrest victory in an untenable position only through the massive airlift of arms by the United States. Once again, the US showed that it had the power and the means to determine who will win out in a shooting war in the Middle East.

BIBLIOGRAPHY

Below is a selection of books on the Watergate scandal that the author has found to be illuminating.

Bernstein, Carl and Woodward, Bob, *All the President's Men*, (London: Bloomsbury, 1974).

Chua, Amy, *Day of Empire*, (New York: Doubleday, 2007).

Dean, John, *Blind Ambition*, (New York: Simon Schuster, 1976).

Emery, Fred, *Watergate: The Corruption and Fall of Richard Nixon*, (New York: Touchstone, 1994).

Ehrlichman, John, *Witness to Power: The Nixon Years*, (New York: Pocketbooks, 1982).

Haldeman, HR, *The Haldeman Diaries*, (New York: Berkeley, 1995).

Ji Chaozhu, *The Man on Mao's Right*, (New York: Random House, 2008).

Kissinger, Henry, *The White House Years*, (New York: Little Brown, 1979).

Kissinger, Henry, *Years of Renewal*, (London: Weidenfield & Nicholson, 1999).

Kuttle, Stanley, *Abuse of Power*, (New York: Touchstone, 1997).

MacMillan, Margaret, *Seize the Hour: When Nixon met Mao*, (London: John Murray, 2007).

Nixon, Richard, *RN: The Memoirs of Richard M Nixon*, (New York: Touchstone, 1990).

Nixon, Richard, *Six Crisis*, (New York: Doubleday, 1962).

Sun Tzu [Sunzi], *The Art of War*, (London: Penguin, 2008).

Woodward, Bob, and Bernstein, Carl, *The Final Days*, (London: Pocketbooks, 1976).

ABOUT THE AUTHOR

Name: René Wen Suen Chang
Email: renechang@btinternet.com
Degrees and Qualifications:
BSc (Special) Physiology, King's College, University of London
MB BS, Westminster Medical School, University of London
F.R.C.S. (England), Royal College of Surgeons (England)
Master of Surgery (MS), University of London
Awards:
Entrance Scholarship to Westminster Medical School
Federal Scholarship (Malaysian Government)
Bernard Sunley Research Fellowship, RCS (England)
Present Appointment:
Author and Director of Useful & Fun Things Limited
Past Appointments:
1. Founding Director of Transplantation, St George's Hospital, London
2. Consultant Surgeon, Riyadh Military Hospital, Saudi Arabia
3. Lecturer/Senior Registrar, Academic Surgical Unit, St Mary's Hospital, London.
4. Clinical Tutor (Postgraduate/undergraduate), King Faisal University, Damman, King Saud University, College of Medicine, Riyadh
5. Consultant Transplant Surgeon, St Helier Hospital, Carshalton, Surrey
6. Scientific Advisor/Consultant to 2nd Consensus Conference of the European Society of Intensive Care, Fujisawa GmbH, Eli Lilly, Hoffman La Roche, Glaxo-Wellcome, Qinetiq, Intensive Care National Audit and Research Centre, UK,
7. Chairman, South Thames Transplant Group - 1992-1994
8. Visiting Professor, George Washington University, Washington DC
Teaching Experience (Undergraduate and Postgraduate):
King's College, Strand, University of London
St Bartholomew's, Westminster, St Mary's Hospitals Medical Schools, London, UK
King Saud University Medical School, Riyadh, Saudi Arabia

King Faisal University Colleges of Medicine, Al Khobar, Damman, Saudi Arabia

Conferences and Workshops (Organised):
Monthly Nutrition Support Service Workshop 1980-89
International Symposium on Intensive Care. Riyadh 1982
2nd International Middle East Symposium on Organ Transplantation Riyadh, 1984
Nutritional Care of the Critically Ill Patient. International Symposium at Riyadh 1987
Symposium on End-stage Renal Disease and Renal Transplantation at Riyadh 1988
Symposium - Practical Problems in Transplantation, St George's Hospital, London, 1996

Societies
British Transplantation Society
British Medical Association
Intensive Care Society (U.K.)
European Society of Intensive Care
Society of Critical Care Medicine
American Federation for Clinical Research

Publications and presentations:
Peer reviewed articles and chapters in books on tumour immunology, renal transplantation, surgical nutrition, surgical audit, intensive care, and disaster response planning.
Interviewed by international (Germany, Austria, Singapore, Malaysia, Australia, USA, Canada), national (UK) and local radio (London, Scotland), television stations (BBC Today, GMTV, BBC News 24, Cologne TV) and newspapers (Times, Independent, Guardian, Telegraph, Evening Standard, Daily and Sunday Express, Daily Mail, Sun, Stern, Frankfurt Zeitung, Straits Times, Sydney Morning Herald).

Educational Videos:
I scripted, directed, and produced the following educational videos:
A day in the life of a Nutrition Support Service.
Renal transplantation in Saudi Arabia.
Carry On Feeding.

Computer Programs:

I designed and wrote the following computer software programs:-
Editorial Office Manager Version 1.0. 1984.
Nutrition Support Service Manager Version 2.0. 1986.
Riyadh ICU Program Version 2.30 2004
Renal Data Manager Version 3.0 2009
Recent Books.

Scalpel in the Sand (2011)

Watergate - The Political Assasination (2012)

Where to find Rene Chang online

Website: http://usefulandfunthings.com or http://uftpress.com

http://www.smashwords.com/profile/view/renechang

René's memoirs - *Scalpel in the Sand - Memoirs of a surgeon in Saudi Arabia* is available in print and also as an eBook. The ebook is available in many different formats such as Nook (Barnes & Noble), Sony eReader, Kindle, Nobo (WH Smith), etc. and is available to purchase online at Amazon in most countries. For your convenience both the UK and US URLs are given.

United Kingdom

http://www.amazon.co.uk/Scalpel-in-the-Sand-ebook/dp/B0058HUFYQ/ref=sr_1_2?s=books&ie=UTF8&qid=1336521793&sr=1-2

United States

http://www.smashwords.com/books/view/72611

http://www.amazon.com/Scalpel-in-the-Sand-ebook/dp/B0058HUFYQ/ref=sr_1_1?ie=UTF8&qid=1336521158&sr=8-1

The print version of *Scalpel in the Sand* (9 x 6 inches, 244 pages with 24 plates, ISBN 9780956911902) is also available for purchase in both the UK and the US.

UK- http://www.amazon.co.uk/Scalpel-Sand-Memoir-Surgeon-Arabia/dp/0956911900/ref=sr_1_1?ie=UTF8&qid=1339017374&sr=8-1

US - http://www.amazon.com/Scalpel-Sand-Memoir-Surgeon-Arabia/dp/0956911900/ref=sr_1_2?ie=UTF8&qid=1336521158&sr=8-2

Reviews of Scalpel in the Sand

La Vaughn Kemnow - Amazon.co.uk - 19 Mar 2012

Captivating

The richness of this narrative is enhanced by the many details of the life of an expatriate living and working in Saudi Arabia. Vignettes of his personal life woven seamlessly in with details of his professional life make a rich tapestry that lures the reader to read just one more page...then one more... Detailed accounts of local customs and mores are fascinating to read, and elicit the feeling that the reader is there, experiencing the culture right along with the author. The details presented of his experiences (sights, sounds, smells, feelings, etc.) provide depth and breadth that draw the reader in. His experience as a surgeon living and working in Saudi Arabia enhanced Chang's professional development and enriched his growth as a person. Part of this growth encompassed essential components such as awareness of self; awareness of his own strengths, weaknesses and limitations; and adapting to local conditions. It is an altogether captivating and informative book.

Kim Wherry Amazon.co.uk - 17 Dec 2011

Read This Book!

Author, Rene Chang bases his book 'Scalpel in the Sand' over a ten year span spent advancing his career working as a Surgeon in Saudi Arabia. Fragments of the authors life in Malaysia and the United Kingdom are integrated throughout the book developing a nice intersection of cultures.

The book takes you on a journey on a road that is less travelled. It reflects upon numerous events happening within the workplace as well as sharing stories of travels to a different country and adapting to new cultures and ways of life.

The journey deals with aspirations, frustrations, emotions, motivations, commitments and raises your awareness to possibilities in life. The events that take place within the memoir are a beautiful balance of both professional and personal experiences.

This is a thoroughly enjoyable book. This book would be extremely beneficial to those within the Medical Profession. I myself am not from the Medical Profession and found this to be an engaging and enjoyable book. It is easy to read, honest and a great story.

Stoke Dry - Amazon.co.uk - 27 Sep 2011

Insight

I was a medical student at the same time as Mr Chang in a different Medical School. I never thought about how the students from overseas were feeling, now I know. The same discrimination, which also applied to women at the time, continued after graduation and led to Saudi Arabia. The author was well placed to understand the lot of women in Saudi Arabia. Mr Chang is very open about his thoughts and feelings on this subject and it is this, together with the chapter on how his family came to be in Malaysia, then England, which makes it such a fascinating book to read. For an non surgeon it also provides insight into how a surgeon trains and develops into a different sort of human being. It is probably best read by people with some medical knowledge, but there is plenty in it for those without.

Hew Foo Hin - Amazon.com - 28 Oct 2011

The good surgeon

This truly is remarkable. A little Chinese boy from Kuala Lumpur, in the fifties attended a Catholic School. In the sixties, studied in a university in London and became a surgeon. However he could not find a job in London, and in 1979 landed a job in Saudi Arabia, as a surgeon. Turned out that this was the best thing to have happened, as he was thrust into an environment where everything was possible. This is his story of his 10 years as a surgeon in the Riyadh Military Hospital. And what do we know about the Saudis? This is a good place to start. You will be surprised.
Do not miss the chapter on Idiosyncrasies and Oddities. It has some revealingly funny anecdotes. Who do you think was the greatest tourist agent ever? Find out in this chapter. Those of us who are thinking of a job overseas, this book is definitely required reading

Watergate - The Political Assassination

René Chang

Made in the USA
Columbia, SC
21 November 2020